corrupted
TORMENT

ISLA HARDING

CORRUPTED TORMENT

OF CAPTURE AND COERCION
BOOK ONE

ISLA HARDING

Written by - Isla Harding
Cover Design by - Dez at Pretty in Ink Creations
Editing & Formatting by - K.L. Taylor-Lane

Captured as a child, Nixi never stood a chance. Brought to an island filled with fear. It doesn't take her long to understand. When the sirens ring out; there's only one thing to do.

Run.

She's not the only one running. The guys are too and when they meet; their world is going to ignite.

Dedicated to all those who have been imprisoned in their lives in all senses of the word.
From people who have been trapped inside an endless loop of anxiety, depression, and other mental health issues; to those who are trapped in thankless and toxic relationships.
This is for you, let books be your escape, enjoy a little slice away from reality.

NOTE FROM THE AUTHOR

Corrupted Torment is a prequel novella containing multiple triggers that are listed in the back of the book and are also available to view on the author's socials.

Please know your own limits, if you have no triggers then dive on in; if you are cautious, I do advise checking them first.
This book has some very heavy themes throughout, so please do heed my warning and check those TWs if you are worried.

My brain is warped, okay?

Continue on at your own risk.

This is a dark why choose romance containing MM. This

is a Novella meaning it is a short story and does end on a small cliffhanger.

Please note this book is written in British English. We like the letter U and hate the letter Z. Things may read a little differently to what you are used to. However, if you do find anything you think is a genuine error, please, please do let me know. Thank you!

PROLOGUE

RAFFERTY

Age Twenty-Six

"Do you understand me, Little Seductress?"

My Wildcat's body trembles at my whispered words, her lust-filled eyes staring up at me as we stand shrouded in the darkness. It's exhilarating watching as her pupils dilate with each thought that creeps through her. Desire vibrating, almost palpable in the air.

We both know the consequences of this, but I need her decision to be clear. Her body already screaming the outcome, but I need her mind to catch up. At her nod, I let a feral grin touch my lips. We both knew that she would say yes, but I had to give her this choice. She could decide to stay, to say no, and I wouldn't blame her. But my Wildcat is used to *easy* not being an option, and she makes it clear that easy is the last thing she wants.

My Little Seductress runs.

There's no method in her direction as she rushes from me, frenzied and chaotic. My eyes trace her delicate frame as she crashes through the undergrowth, and I can't help the chuckle that pulls from my lips. I love seeing her like this.

Her tangled mess of auburn waves snag in low-hanging branches as she passes, but she doesn't seem to care as she dashes past. Her bare feet slap on the dry compacted mud and the sound echoes through the quiet night, twisting with her joyous laughter. She's so unlike her usual self. Tonight, her journey is unplanned, wild, and free-spirited. There is no chance I won't catch her, and she knows it.

The only difference is, Wildcat wants to be caught this time.

The taste of her blood on my lips has my cock twitching as I follow my own slow path. Stalking her silently, watching her pale form in the distance but never getting too close. Surrounded by densely packed trees, moonlight only sneaks through in dappled spotlights that I easily avoid.

Her luminous skin and white dress are a beacon in the night for me to trail, her usual tricks not in place to cloak herself. Directing her stormy blue eyes into the distance, her pace slows to a jog, the moonlight casting shadows over her features as she turns her head. Wildcat doesn't even notice me as she sweeps her gaze across my still-form hidden in the pitch black of the night.

I hear her let out a huff of breath as she speeds up once more. It seems my Little Seductress is frustrated. It amuses me she thought I would let this be over so quickly. How could she possibly forget I enjoy the hunt? Right now, she isn't playing fair, giving in too easily. Such a needy little thing.

She's not even thought about it as she runs from me. Hasn't taken in the consequences of her actions. Just like me, she knows we need this release. This game we have played for years has new rules now.

Today we are going to learn them.

As time goes on, I watch as the panic sets in, settling into her. Her shoulders rising as the tension builds. My Little Seductress probably doesn't even realise when she pulls her thick lip between her teeth. I've already warned her about that; I'll have to remind her that those lips are mine later.

She whips her head around, looking in every direction before stopping her run. Stress overriding her senses and I'm intrigued to know what thoughts are circling through her mind. She searches for cover but quickly spots her problem. The only place to hide is in the trees above, and her energy is waning.

I know exactly how to resolve that. Fear does wonderful things for adrenaline levels; I'm sure Wildcat won't mind when she realises what I'm doing. In fact, I'm sure she'll be exhilarated. I slink closer to her, my feet placed strategically as always to make no sound. The night is deathly silent, making the pounding of her heart-beat loud to my sensitive ears as her anxiety creeps.

I stand directly behind my Wildcat. My cock thickens, knowing what is to come as I reach my hands out. Deftly, I wrap one hand around her mouth, catching her scream. The other; I lock around her slender waist, dragging her back into my chest.

Where she belongs.

I can't resist breathing in her earthy scent with hues of vanilla. It's intoxicating. My Little Seductress struggles, kicking her legs out into the air, and a dark laugh escapes me. This life isn't an easy one, certainly not one for the weak. Many have perished on the islands on which we live, but here she is, still standing strong. Always fighting like she should be, even against me.

Difference is, I won't ever let my obsession perish, she is mine and I will always protect her.

"I told you if you ran, I would always find you."

CHAPTER 1

NIXI

Age Twelve

Nightmare turns into reality as my eyes fight to open. I regret it instantly as the scorching sun blares above me. I blink my eyes shut, trying to clear the orbs dotting my vision. My body is so drained of energy, even that slight movement is hard to accomplish.

After several minutes, I'm able to reopen my eyelids. I lift my arm and notice my pale skin has turned red from the burning sun. I look around and take in my unknown surroundings. It could be straight from someone's dreams about an idyllic paradise. I'm on a beach, with waves of cool, clean water tauntingly rippling towards me. Where I was from, a beach like this would've been full of people. Men and women sunbathing, families with children playing in the sea or building sandcastles.

I'm alone on this beach.

Other than the lapping of the waves, the silence brings a chill to my overheated skin. Something feels wrong. On the horizon, nothing but the ocean lies ahead of me. No land or even a sign of a ship is in sight. Above, no planes appear in the sky. Behind me lies a dense landscape of trees that edge right onto the sand. No man-made footpaths or buildings. It's as if this place is untouched, but I know that can't be the truth. Otherwise, how did I end up here?

I don't remember.

The thought is frightening and made worse by my body's exhaustion. I'm so tired. It takes several long minutes to have enough strength to crawl my way to the shade of the treeline. Here I curl up to rest while my reddened skin throbs, itchy and sore with heat. My throat is parched, desperate for even just a taste of water.

"Told you she couldn't hack it," a woman's voice gruff with annoyance speaks above me. "She'll be a drain. Just leave her there." I don't move as she speaks. My head is unbearably heavy.

Something jabs sharply into my side. I'm pushed roughly by a foot and turned onto my back. It hurts, but I squint my eyes open. I look up at two figures hovering above me, both haloed by light. Letting out a disgruntled noise, I lift my heavy head and try to peer closer, but can only make out their outlines. The bright sunlight obscuring my vision.

"Don't be like that, Aggs. If it were up to you, no one would be let in," a softer voice replies. "She's just a kid."

I hadn't heard either of them approach. Had I passed out, or had they been watching me all along? I'm not sure I want to know. Either way, the first woman–Aggs–seems to be happy enough to leave me here.

"Let's get the girl up. A bit of food an' water an' she'll be fine. Can't tell me you weren't the same your first day," the nicer of the pair continues. The other woman scoffs in response.

My body raises upwards as the two women drape my arms around their shoulders. On either side of me, they each grab hold of my waist and move me to a standing position. I'm an unbalanced mess, the two of them holding most of my weight, but I try my best to remain as steady as I can.

"'Least she's fucking light. Better not be like the last one."

"She's young. I don't think it'll be a problem. Come on, kid, we've got you now."

I struggle to keep moving—trying to stay upright with the women's help—while feeling the scorching burn of the sand beneath my sinking feet. Soon, it turns to much cooler, dry earth and leaves a welcome relief on the bottoms of my sore feet. The occasional rock stabs its way into my sole, but I'm almost too numb to notice.

Keeping one foot in front of the other is all I can concentrate on. My eyes are unfocused as we travel past the sand and through the trees, away from the lapping water of the beach. As I start to trip and stumble, the women's arms keep me in their firm grip. They continue to speak, their words drifting off into a mumbled background noise.

Blackness curls at the edges of my vision as my legs drag limply behind me, scuffing the tops of my feet over rough debris. These two strangers carry me to an unknown fate. Finally, I succumb to the darkness, letting it cocoon me softly in its embrace.

When I wake, an older girl is peering down at me. I startle and push myself upright on my elbows, scrabbling back away from her on my bum. My movements are awkward with my legs trapped in a tangled blanket.

Her lips curve into an amused smirk as she flicks short brown hair from her eyes. Looking at her more intently, I realise she can't be more than a few years older than me.

She picks something up from beside her and shakes it. Liquid sloshes inside and my dry lips part. Thirst overrides every other emotion, my fear dissolving. There is just a desperate need and I'm in complete thrall of what she holds.

"Here, drink some water, kid," she says, shuffling

towards me and thrusting the canteen into my chest with force. I don't even care. I grasp the thing with frantic hands, twisting the cap before gulping at the cool water greedily. It spills over my cracked lips and it's heavenly, better than anything I've ever tasted.

Slowly, it quells the dehydration that had taken over my body, but a cry spills from me as she snatches the canteen back. I need that; I'm not finished. I'm still so thirsty. Could I have been out in the sun without water for much longer than I'd realised? No wonder I had passed out.

"Don't waste it, you stupid cow. You should've sipped the damn water anyway. Over there, follow that path. Get your own supplies," she snarls, pointing vaguely behind her. She goes to stand, but I somehow grip onto her wrist before she does.

"Where are we? What is this place?" I try to plead with her. She pushes my hand away, shaking her head before rising to her feet, staring cooly down at me with piercing green eyes and I deflate. Sure that she is not going to answer, my body sags and I look away from her penetrating stare. Unable to focus on her any longer.

"I don't know what this is, or where we are. I just do as I'm told, and if you're smart, you'll do the same. Now get up, kid. You need three dresses, a sleeping bag, a water canteen, and enough rations for yourself for a week. Those need to be brought to the main fire pit. We divvy the food up there. You get them from the warehouse down that trail. Got it?"

I nod, it's more than I expected. Tiredness shoots through my aching limbs as I struggle to stand, making it to my hands and knees. She nods back, offering me no help before walking away.

"Oh, and don't take more than you're rationed; you'll regret that." Her final warning shout is called over her shoulder, leaving me alone in this strange place. She doesn't even turn her head as I begin to softly cry, large wet tears rolling down my cheeks.

It takes a long, painful time for me to get up, and it terrifies me at how weak I am, how vulnerable. Plenty of others are walking around, but not one person comes to help me. I seem to be in some kind of shanty town, well, a village. Women peek out of run-down-looking shacks but look away when I try to catch their eye. I'm just a kid, but it doesn't appear to make a difference. They want nothing to do with me.

I trek past the homes, quickly realising that no one wants to help me. As more people—all young girls and women—choose to ignore my presence, I feel the hiccupping sob erupt from within me. I'm so scared and I don't know where I am. I can't contain it as my crying becomes a noisy mess of snivelling tears.

Panic filters through my body and I shake with each step I take. The pressure of so many pairs of eyes upon me is akin to daggers stabbing me in the back. A betrayal yet to be made, or one they make with each fumbling step I take.

I stumble, somehow catching myself before I fall. The

snickers that follow let me know they saw. They are nothing but bullies who find my pain amusing. Do the people here just prey on the weak? Their eyes observe me, assess me, and looking back, I can't see a drop of kindness in sight. What made them this way?

I hate this.

Growing up in the foster system, my life had never been some fairy tale. At least the people there were mostly nice, much nicer than they are here, wherever here is. Sure, there'd been one or two people I hadn't liked, but this is on a whole other level.

At least at the group home, people had my back. They met all my major needs, and I really couldn't complain. They even gave me an allowance. Sure, I needed to fend for myself often enough, and maybe I had grown up quicker than some of the other kids, but I've never had it bad. I just know more about the world. Book smarts might not be my thing, but ask me to look after the younger kids, or do the washing. I'm your girl. Well, I was anyway.

Here, I'm already segregated and alone, without an offer of help or relief from this miserable place. I want my best friend, Zee. We shared a room, trading secrets and comfort in the night. We have this book of poems—one Zee came to the home with—we always said we would write our own someday. I hope she's okay. Will I find those sorts of comforts ever again?

I don't understand this mentality. Is this some kind of ritual teasing, like some sort of test I need to pass? Can I go back home? Do any of the women know how they came to be here? Are there any men? How long have they been here? Why watch me sleep if they didn't want to help? Why bother even bringing me from the beach at all?

My head is a blur of wild thoughts. All reaching and rising to be up front and centre, a swirling mass of confusion. I want to scream, to make the chaos tumbling around inside me stop. It's always been this way: lost inside my mind. Right now, overriding them all, shouting loudly inside me, is my thirst.

I need to move, to get water, or I could die.

Scanning the area again, I know I can't afford to fall apart completely right now. I have to focus on controlling my breathing. A whimper escapes my lips, but I try to remain strong. Ignoring everyone around me as my stomach cramps in protest and hunger twists my insides. Concentrating again on the direction that was pointed out to me, I finally spot what could possibly be a pathway in the trees, and I shuffle onwards.

The tremor in my steps is slowing me down, but I keep walking with my head held high, despite the tears sliding down my cheeks. I've never felt this vulnerable and shaky in my life, but I have no choice but to keep going. Thirsty, hungry, and exhausted, I traipse one footfall at a time until I reach the path I'm sure I am supposed to follow.

Mapped out by the tread of feet, I follow the dirt path, thankful for the shade of the trees on either side as I trudge on. I don't know how long I walk; I only know it wouldn't take anywhere near as long if I were in better condition. Worn down by time, the pathway is wider than I would've guessed. It looks like it allows multiple people to walk alongside one another. A few women pass me and walk back towards the camp, completely ignoring me like everyone else, and I just keep moving, focused on the path ahead.

The trees start to thin down, and in the distance, I finally glimpse my first look of what I can only guess is the warehouse. Large and looming, the building is not at all what I'd expected in such a desolate place. As I draw closer, my eyes widen at the sight of it overlooking the beach. The path continues straight to a doorway on the left of the dark grey building, made from stone and wood. My shoulders tense as I creep towards it. My fear ratchets back up at the thought of what's inside.

"Move."

An elbow jabs painfully into my side. There's hate in the woman's dark eyes, and it fills me with unease. I don't know what I have done to offend her. She glowers, looking me up and down like I'm a piece of meat before continuing on, a sneer on her lips.

Was I walking too slowly? Glancing at the path, I know she could easily have gone around me. Perhaps she needs me to hurry to catch her up? I don't know why she felt the need to hurt me to get my attention. Clutching my now aching side, I make myself move more swiftly to chase after her into the gloomy warehouse. I don't want to upset her further.

I don't want to make any enemies here. Worried it's already far too late for that, I bite the corner of my lip anxiously as I walk closer. Sweat drips down my back and body trembles as each step I take amps up my nerves. This is worse than going up to senior school, especially when the risks are so much higher.

I push open the door slowly, uncertainly peeking my head around the door before I enter. I don't see the woman, but I am stunned to find the rows upon rows of supplies. It's enough to last the people here for years. Blankets, clothes, and food line the walls, along with enough metal and wood to build several shelters. It makes me wonder why they didn't just set up camp here. Why are these things supplied at all? It's basic, but it's all vital.

"Glad you could finally make it. I wasn't sure you would. I'm Aggs."

Her voice echoes from behind me, making me jump. I spin, letting out a whimper as I find her staring at me with a nasty tilt to her lips. Aggs. The woman who found me on the beach, the one who wanted to leave me to die. I hadn't been able to make her out earlier in the harsh sun, but her size and power would have frightened me on a good day, let alone today.

It seems the woman was here for me after all.

Alone.

"Grab a rucksack. Let's set you up."

Her eyes track my every move, and I can't help the creeping tremor that shakes through my body as I follow her instructions. I anxiously keep my distance, feeling like

I'm too close to a snake about to strike. My side aches from the blow she has already doled out to me, and I'm scared that's not even close to the worst thing she will do to me.

I think she's the one bringing out the worst in the women. She's at least the one who has the power to control them, to rule with an iron fist. The thought is terrifying. I'm going to need to learn to lie low and to keep to myself.

Unease curls through me as I look around. The weight of suspicion lingers heavily in the air, but I don't understand why. I've been here for four days in this shanty village on an island no one wants to speak about. Reality is a long-forgotten dream that's left me captive to this nightmare.

Here, the homes are a mishmash of large scraps of wood and metal. It's just enough protection from the worst of the elements, placed amongst the base of trees. The trunks look like they keep the homes as sturdy as can be, while being held together with thick rope. At least that's all I can see is holding the things together, but I suspect it must be more. I haven't figured that part out yet, and the people here aren't too forthcoming.

Although the camp isn't an immense area, the place holds at least a hundred of these little shacks. They're barely big enough to lie flat in a sleeping bag and store our few items of clothing. To be honest, they're more like uneven, decrepit mausoleums settled among the trees. They're left to rot, decay, and rust. Some have real-looking doors with hinges creaking from age, but most only have a sheet of plastic covering to protect the occupants from the outside.

I've only just begun to create my own. The pieces are leaning together against a strong-looking oak tree. Its sturdy branches are reaching up to the sky and are easy enough to climb if I ever felt the need. It's a reminder of one in the garden from the group home. It had been my safe space amongst the leaves. Currently, I have a wooden base, a plastic sheet, and two metal walls picked out, but have so far not started construction.

I've had to go back to the warehouse a few times already. On the third day, after giving myself a day's rest, I dragged the beginning of my new home back. I didn't know just how much effort the heavy scraps would take to move.

Panting with exertion, my face undoubtably red, I struggled, heaving, pulling and dragging the hefty panels. Others laughed behind their hands and whispered to one another as I held back my tears and the frustration thrumming through me. No one would help me.

Well, not until Fliss came along from a scouting trip today. Without a thought, she helped me heft up the large piece of metal I'd been struggling with, and we carried it between us to my chosen location.

Now, I'm sitting at one of the campfires to warm my chilled bones as the night-time temperature drops. Sitting next to me is Fliss, the nicer of the two women who'd brought my unconscious body back from the beach.

Fliss seems to have taken a liking to me, and after her help today, I'm eternally grateful for her generous spirit. The fire flickers, catching the light in her rich brown eyes that reflect the dancing flame right back. Maybe it's just because she helped me, but she seems so different from everyone else here.

Her kindness and beauty are a balance of one another. Her olive complexion and black hair are a striking combination along with her sharp cheekbones. She's way older than me, in her twenties, and has gained respect that I could never hope to earn.

Since she helped me this morning, things have been a little lighter. Everyone seems to respect Fliss, and from watching her, it really appears like she cares. I get the impression she's someone I could trust, and I think Zee would approve of her too. Not that I'll ever see my best friend again. At least I assume I won't.

I bring my knees up to my chest and wrap my arms around them. Nothing here makes sense to me. I'm nothing like Fliss. My hair is a tangled brown mess, my eyes are a boring blue, and I'm still a child. I'm not exactly dumb but I'm neither smart nor quick-witted either and so far, I only feel like a burden.

I don't understand why I am here, or how I came to be here. The only thing I can guess is that I'm on some insane reality TV show. One with only young girls and women. I've asked questions since I've been here, but no one's been open to giving me any answers.

They *must* know something.

"Fliss?"

She hums her acknowledgement.

"Please, I need to know. What is this place? Why am I here?"

Pity enters her gaze before she looks away from me. I watch as she swallows, and I can see the thoughts flitting through her mind as she takes her time to answer. She stiffens, and the morsel of hope I had for information disappears at the lie I can sense she's ready to spout.

"I don't know what this place is. None of us do. We don't know why we're here or what they want. It just is this way," she speaks softly. It's the non-answer I'd expected, one I'd received through clenched teeth and glowering eyes when I'd asked the others.

Disappointment fills me. I'd hoped this time I'd get more. Fliss isn't like them. I look up at her, imploring her to continue. She's reluctant and I'm positive it's all I will get out of her, at least for tonight.

"This place is hell." The raw truth escapes her lips on a sigh, her eyes downcast as she continues on.

"We've always been sent new girls—and always kids— every few months. Some we find on the beach. Some we don't. We always try our best to help them, but we never know when they're coming."

Her words are steady, but Fliss refuses to meet my eyes and I know why. I heard Aggs that day, and I know at least one thing she says is a lie. Sometimes they get there in time; sometimes they just leave them there to die.

Aggs is a harsh woman, and an unofficial leader. A figurehead here. What Aggs says is law. It seems my face doesn't fit; she's certainly taken an instant dislike to me. I'm an outsider until she says otherwise. I have yet to understand if this pack mentality has reason and what makes Aggs so powerful in this community, and I'm scared to find out. Things are bad enough as it is. The others follow in her wake without thought, reason, or logic.

All except Fliss.

Not once has she taken any notice of the distrustful eyes lingering on me as we've walked around camp today. She didn't let the hateful stares bring her to anger as she gave me my ration of food at dinner. Fliss merely tuts as some completely turn their backs on me. She just dismisses their antics as we warm ourselves by the fire.

I can't stand the secrets and lies though. Unease churns inside me. There's so much I don't know, so much I don't understand.

A blaring sound rings out, shrieking across the village, stirring chaotic movement in its wake. Women and girls start to run in different directions, each knowing its meaning. Birds fly from the trees above from fright, cawing into the night sky. They join the sirens in a symphony of terror. I cover my ears and watch in strange fascination as one by one the women disappear into the cover of trees or into the shelter of their homes.

I rise to my feet, chasing Fliss and knowing for certain she'll tell me what to do and what's happening. Sprinting, I follow close behind towards her home, my bare feet pounding on the cracked earth beneath me. She goes inside, and her hazel eyes catch mine as she turns. Sympathy and pity shine through as she closes the door on me.

My breath stutters. That can't be right.

I reach her door in seconds and pound on it. I know I could force my way in, but that wouldn't be right. Why won't she answer? Why won't she let me in?

"Run, kid. It's the only way now," her hissed words come through the door. This makes no sense. I thought she was my friend.

I take a step back from her door, then another. A root catches my foot, and I come crashing to the floor, landing on my elbows. I let out a yelp as my ankle twists and I rub lightly at the painful throb. Once again, I'm injured and alone. I rise and move aimlessly; I have nowhere else to go, nowhere to hide. My home is in pieces, still yet to be built. The only thing I can think to do is keep warm as I limp my way over to the closest campfire.

It feels like someone has cut off my oxygen as breathing becomes difficult. I try not to let the panic overwhelm me and take in deep breaths to calm my thudding heart. It's an impossible feat as I try to imagine what has these women so frightened.

The longer I wait, I swear I make out monsters hiding in the darkness of my surroundings. Ones that prowl through the forest landscape of this island. With only the campfire's eerie dancing shadows that slowly burn down to embers combined with the trilling sirens for company, I stay immobile, anticipating the worst.

Sound stops, sudden and abrupt, only the silence of the night can be heard for achingly long seconds. Then the distant wailing screams of fear. I can only remain frozen to see what horror awaits me tonight.

CHAPTER 2

RAFFERTY

Age Eight

I kick my little legs back and forth on the branch of the tree while watching my brothers fight with wild abandon below. None of them have bothered to look up. They don't use logic when the rules are laid out. My brothers use brute force rather than brains. Not me though; I know they will get sleepy eventually.

The fight is to be the last one standing—not who wins the most rounds. All I need to do is to knock out whoever won the fight before I come down. They will be tired and weak, and I will have much more of a chance.

It's not a fair fight. It's okay though; I know how to play dirty.

I see the Doctor from my perched spot. He is not to be confused with a daddy; he is not that to us. No, he is just Doctor. A man with blue eyes, a harsh face, brown hair and a boring white outfit. Always white. His smile is something more predatory, baring his teeth in malicious intent. Though sometimes he will congratulate us on doing well in our games, rewarding us for our success.

He likes to watch the games.

I know he's seen me. He's taking notes on the fighting, writing notes on each of my brothers as they are defeated. He doesn't like me much. Told me until I use my brawn, I'll amount to nothing. He thinks his stupid jacket makes him look so smart, but it doesn't.

Strength doesn't mean everything, and I'll prove it.

I'm the youngest, and some of my brothers are near enough teenage boys. If I tried to fight, I would have lost already. In my books, that makes my brain a massive advantage. As I watch over the fight, I place bets with myself on who will win based on the probability of their skills. My bunkmate has been teaching me. He's a whiz at maths.

Looking at the fight below, Devon will probably be the overall contender for me to defeat. At eleven years old, his anger is twisted in with his speed and determination to win. It's a deadly mix, and as he grows older, his skills will only continue to thrive.

Quietly, I slink down the tree. I watch my black-haired brother fight what he reckons to be the last sibling between himself and victory. I am careful to avoid his notice. The grunt and telltale thud of a body hits the ground.

Out of nowhere, he appears, fists already raised. My head pounds at the single punch he slams into my cheek. His eyes are black, filled with darkness as the malicious grin of victory spreads across his face. It's the last thing I see before I hit the floor in defeat.

I was kidding myself to believe I could beat Devon.

I never really stood a chance.

AGE TEN

Outside the perimeter of our facility home, me and my brothers walk in single file through the trees along the stone path. Large drops of water slowly drip from the trees above as dark clouds line the sky.

A rainstorm has just passed, but it's far from over as we splash on the puddled walkway, cleaning our muddied boots. It makes me smile briefly, the thought of actually being a kid for one glorious second as I stamp my foot down just a little bit harder than necessary. The slap round the back of my head from an accompanying nurse is worth it for that precious moment.

Our Doctor leads us onwards, only stopping to point his arm out into the woodland. Oh goody, a treasure hunt of doom. As I approach, he gives me a smile full of gleaming teeth, a grin for each of us as we pass. The look is way more unsettling to me than whatever it is he's trying to portray.

Knowing him, it's exactly what he wants.

As we trek into the wilderness of the island in a long snakelike queue, I keep my eyes peeled for whatever challenge they have set us. I know full well it could be anything. Over the years, I have lost nine brothers to this place. Five have died from the trials we have been given.

An elbow rams painfully into my gut, and I let out a squeak. I need to tread carefully; things have become so much more dangerous than they once were. Now it's become a challenge just to stay alive. Knowing it is pointless going against the bigger boy, I ignore Devon as he stalks past. He is the worst of them all.

As I grow, the time for fun is less and less. It's not something I question, it's just a part of growing up. The games we play have become more lethal. They have had their consequences; ones I'm pretty sure are intentional. As things have become more savage, the more Devon enjoys inflicting his brutality. In his vicious mindset, he delights in others' terror, hunting down victims like a monster in the night.

Never his own suffering though.

Devon thirsts to dole out the pain to anyone who crosses his path. His black eyes lighten with a spark of madness every time he drives in the knife. As he listens to the screams, it fills something deep inside him. It doesn't matter if it's friend or foe; no one can truly escape his sights.

The other four of my nine brothers lost their lives because of Devon's blood lust.

One day he'll get his. Until then, I need to take the blows I can and avoid any major damage. I can't be seen to fight back and give him the excuse to do me actual harm. Devon has made his mission to hunt me clear and not just inside the games. He sees me as weak, something I desperately want to change, if only to get his attention away from me.

I watch as Devon makes his way to the front of our pack of brothers, each earning their own jab, punch or kick on the way. He spares no one of his wrath. As if the sky itself feels his madness, it darkens, eclipsing out the sun with clouds.

It's strange to watch him. Something new, something *other* about him has been happening. It's like he is evolving. Devon was always quick, but now he's faster than ever. His strength is almost inhuman, along with his growing volatile mentality. It's very peculiar.

He's only thirteen, but I'm confident he could defeat fully trained men. It scares me.

No, *he* scares me.

I catch sight of long bright material flapping in the wind, knotted high above in the treetops. Whispers break out ahead and I know the first of my brothers must have made it to the rules of today's game. As the first of my brothers make their way to the trees, I curse. I don't have time to waste waiting for everyone before me.

I need to calculate a positive outcome. I look above, attempting to count how many of the colourful markers there are when a flash of lighting illuminates up the sky. Rumbles of thunder follows quickly after. Decision made by the impending rain, I start to race around my brothers to the front of the line. A white beacon of paper shines from within the darkness of the trees.

Like the lightning gave its permission to the sky, cracking open the clouds, the downpour begins. I barely acknowledge its fall as I rush past my other brothers. I ignore their outraged shouts for cutting the queue as I reach my goal.

Laminated paper, a telltale sign the doctors had known of the oncoming storm, holds today's fate. Beneath lies a wooden box, intricate with carvings and far too beautiful to be left to the elements. I skim the note, breath hitching in revelation. They want us to make a choice. One I already know is no one's choice but Devon's.

. . .

To my boys – as you may have noticed, situated above you are multiple markers. There is, in fact, enough for one marker each. The aim of the game is to ensure that all sixty-three are retrieved. Only by putting all the markers inside the box below will you be allowed back home.

However, I consider for you to accomplish so little would be rather disappointing for such a talented bunch of individuals such as yourselves. When I know you are capable of so much more than that.

I suggest instead you make a sport of it. Let's see who can and can't get a marker, by any means necessary. A game of capture multiple flags so to speak. This game, if you choose to accept it, will end at dawn. How many can you get by morning light? You must remain in the trees for your flag to be counted.

I will note we predict the weather to become somewhat brutal in the next few hours, and that may result in casualties. We will not provide assistance to injuries until the challenge is over.

The decision is yours.

We will, as always, be watching.

We are completely screwed.

Others taking my lead rush up beside me, jostling me out of the way, uncaring as mud splashes over us. I move out of their way before I become trampled in the crush of bodies now attempting to learn the rules. My brothers have never understood the value of teamwork. In seconds, one could shout out the instructions for us all to hear.

Not once has it happened.

Shaking my head in frustration, I turn, following those before me. I peer upwards for a treetop without a figure already making their way towards a marker. The only way to succeed in this game is to gain all the flags I can, even if it's just one. Then I can make use of my smaller stature to hide within the leafy branches.

Devon will want nothing but bloodshed. A game that should have been something simple despite the thunderstorm has just turned deadly. The race to gain control over a marker is my only chance to win, but the risk now is so much higher. If you don't win, if you don't succeed, they class you as weak. To be seen as weak, well, it makes life unbearable, and I need to change that.

I start my steady climb, being patient on the wet bark as the rain pours above me. When my muscles begin to ache, I push myself higher and higher, ignoring the burn. Knowing if I give in, I have lost, and they will once again see me as a weak link. I keep my eyes peeled for my brothers. I can't let them catch me; the last thing I need is to endure a fall.

My muscles tense as I catch a flash of someone moving above me. I'm sure I must be as high as the clouds up here, but truthfully, I'm barely halfway up. The pressure of another crossing my path is immense, not knowing if they are an ally or foe. Not entirely certain of who can be trusted.

Pressing myself into the trunk of the tree, I stay as still as possible, hoping not to be seen as I watch a blonde-haired brother leap from branch to branch. Jumping across from one tree to the next with ease. His moves are impressive; I doubt I could ever achieve them.

We each have our skills and as much as I'd love to learn them all, I have yet to take that leap of faith. I much prefer my logic. I don't trust my body to have the strength to jump or have the agility to land with such ease. As my brother launches himself further from my view, I maintain my upward path.

A fork of lightning hits too close for my liking and the instant roar of thunder is loud, making me jump. I only just catch my foot from sliding and I gulp in a heaving breath of relief. The higher up I go, the more exposed I am and the riskier it becomes. The wind is stronger up here, and the branches sway with the ebb and flow of the storm. It is why the doctors have placed the markers in these trees.

What is the challenge without the danger?

Of course, they didn't put them up here themselves. Most likely, they made the guards plant them, or possibly drones. I can't picture the guards having the stamina to climb this high. It's different for us. We have been climbing these trees for as long as I can remember.

I hold fast, my hands gripping tightly as I pull myself up higher and higher. The rain is like ice on my skin, but I can't let it deter my steady momentum. Not letting the movement of the tree rocking in the wind scare me as I cling on. I need to do this. I scan around me, even more weary of my brothers at this height. Especially when the noise of the storm blocks out obvious sounds of their movement.

That's when I see it.

The marker, flapping wildly in the gale above. The thing I need to be seen as something other than weak. I'm not far. My body aches, but I can't help the manic grin as I creep up the last two branches, knowing that I'll at least have one of them in my clutches.

Reaching my hand out to claim my prized marker, I feel the shove from behind. I was so close; I never saw him coming. My focus was so fixed on the marker I hadn't checked my surroundings again, so eager to win. A scream tears from my lungs as my stomach plummets along with my own flailing body. Lightning flashes, revealing Devon's taunting face from above, the echoing thunder drowning out my cries.

Wind whips at my face as I try desperately to right myself and I frantically grip at anything I can to ease my fall. Despite the rain, my hands burn with agonising pain as I grapple for branch after branch. My skin rips and tears with heat, but it is either this or death.

I have no choice at all.

I never do.

The need to survive has my hands gripping tighter, my booted feet kicking into the bark of the trunk, and my back pushes into the closest branch. I take my inner strength from somewhere within as my descent slows and I finally stop about a quarter of the way up the sky-high tree. Panting with exertion, I remain still, catching my breath. Gripping onto the rain-soaked branch for dear life, only letting myself slowly slide down to sit with a leg draped over either side of the branch. Perching myself in the bend of the fork, between bough and trunk.

Whoops and hollers of my brothers' roaring laughter comes from all around, uncaring and spiteful sounds of twisted cruelty. Luckily, there is no sign of them close by and I'm glad for the small reprise to recover. Perhaps they believe I am dead; let them think that for now.

Finally feeling sturdy enough to move my hands away, I spot a yellow stream of material snagged around my thumb. It runs across my palm and tangles into the ripped arm of my jacket. A harsh laugh barks out of me as I realise what I have. Partly fused into the flesh of my hand, shredded and torn in multiple places, is clearly what I had been after. Somehow, in the fall, I had caught hold of and kept my marker.

Pure dumb luck.

A low chuckle huffs from my lips as I stash my prize in my jacket. I raise my hands to the rain, cooling the burning heat of red-raw peeled skin. My eyes narrow when I hear the shuffling of movement above, trying to peer through the heavy rain and prepare myself for trouble.

His cry is so familiar, the only brother I have ever truly

trusted. Terror floods my veins as I witness his body fall towards me from above. His pale hair flapping madly in the wind as his petrified golden eyes meet mine.

He's moving so fast, but his fall is almost directly in my path. He must have followed me up the same tree. I shuffle forward on the branch and brace myself. The pain in my hands means nothing as I stretch out my arm for him. I don't care about my pain so long as I can stop this from happening. I can't lose him.

Our fingers brush.

He keeps on falling.

I couldn't catch him.

I watch in horror as he plummets. He yelps and squeals as he hits branches on the way down, but I refuse to look away. The crack and thud of his final descent has me moving fast. I need to get to him; to help him. My heart breaks in the brief deafening silence, my anguish taking control over me as my body shudders in its weakened defeat.

His scream has my heart thudding back to life as I scramble back down. For just a moment there, I had thought the worst. I had thought he was gone, leaving me behind.

From above comes the howling laughter at my brother's pain. It sickens me. These monsters deserve worse than anything my imagination could come up with. Perhaps this storm raging above can take them all. I just don't understand what happened to them to make them turn so depraved. All I know is I want nothing to do with it, or them.

Slipping and sliding, I reach the ground much slower than I would've liked. Trying my best to go speedily, but not wanting to suffer the same fate at taking a misstep on the sodden branches. I rush to his side, trying not to wretch at the gruesome sight of his bone torn through flesh. His left forearm is completely destroyed. Bloodied white bone peeks out from his skin where it has no business being surrounded by ripped tendons and ligaments.

I feel sick, but I have no time to think about it as I kneel beside my bunkmate, trying to reason what I can do for him now. His face is pale, probably as white as mine is green. No help will come until dawn, which worries me while he is bleeding this badly.

As I watch him, I blindly reach for my pocket, willing the torn material to be strong enough. A marker now turned into a tourniquet; I hope to help save my brother's life. His scream is piercing as I raise his arm even the slightest bit, his panicked eyes finally focusing on me. With the fabric under his arm just above the break, I bind it tightly.

I can only hope the doctors will be able to fix him come morning. Though the scars will haunt him forever. His shrieks turn into whimpers. Red-rimmed, golden eyes move frantically back and forth, yet he sees nothing. I'm pretty sure it's not just his arm I should be worried about, but I have done all I can for now.

My need to win is gone. It doesn't matter to me that I

lost as soon as my feet touched the forest floor. Right now, the only thing that matters is keeping my genuine family safe and alive until dawn. With the moon just rising and the storm only getting worse; I know it's going to be a long night.

"It's going to be okay, Aiden."

CHAPTER 3

DARIO

Age Twelve

Rain drips down my face, hiding the tears drenching my cheeks. I don't know how I wound up here. I just know I'm alone. So alone. I've never been one for outdoors and nature; this place has no signs of anything but. All I've seen is tree after tree after tree. Maybe I'm going around in circles. I don't know, but I've certainly not seen any sign of civilisation anywhere.

I'm still wearing the pyjamas I put on for bed. It's the last thing I remember before waking up here. I remember wishing mum goodnight as I trudged up the stairs, then wrapping myself up warm in PJs blocking the icy chill from the house. I'd then covered myself in blankets before willing sleep to overcome me. The Star Wars pattern seems childish now that I'm out here in the open, and ready for the taking.

Then again, it seems I've already been taken.

It's been a few hours since I woke, and I've walked for what must have been miles. I've seen what I can only assume are footprints, smudged beyond recognition by the weather, but fresh enough not to have washed away entirely. I've also witnessed flashes of movement in the distance and calls in the shadows, but no actual people. There's no one to tell me why I've been brought here.

"Hey," a whispered shout calls.

Startled, I spin and slip slightly in the mud beneath my sock-covered feet. I turn to the voice and catch myself before falling on my arse. It's a boy, but he's older. I take a step backwards, rubbing fruitlessly at my tear-stained face with the sleeve of my top. I know better than to let an older boy see my weakness.

"Stay back," I scream back at him, my words echoing among the trees.

He lifts his hands like he's trying to placate an animal, but I'm not fooled by that. Bigger boys like to play games. I search around me for a weapon, seeing nothing but mud and rain-soaked foliage and twigs.

"Not too loud. I'm just trying to help. I know a place, and a fair few of us guys stay there. We look out for one another." His voice is quiet, soothing. He rubs a hand through his blonde waves, shaking some of the water free. It's in need of a cut, like he's been here a while.

My eyes narrow; I take another step back, trying to work out what game he is playing—if he's playing one at all. I eye the trees surrounding me to be positive that no others are watching and that they aren't hunting in a pack.

"I'm not going to hurt you, but others out there might. Please. Just come with me." He sounds so sincere. His face is so open and full of honesty that my resolve almost breaks. Something inside me is screaming at me to trust him; he's just a boy too. It's not possible for him to be the one to have taken me. He's not one of the older boys who bullied me back home, but the fear inside me as he takes a step towards me overrides all logical thought.

I run.

His shouts follow from behind me, but his words don't register as the world flashes past me. I don't know if he gives chase. My fear insisting I need to move and get away. It's a purely instinctual flight away from potential danger. I run until the breath leaves my lungs, and I hunch over with my hands on my knees, panting from the exertion.

"Hello there, little one."

My body goes tense. The voice is not the boy's. It's older, that of a man's. I fear I've jumped out of the frying pan directly into the fire without the energy to fight. Looking up, I can't see him in the clearing I've stopped in.

The trees bathed in darkness and leaves shelter the trunks from the moon's glow.

Ice floods my veins at my unknown threat. I try to remember some techniques that I have been taught to calm the emotions down, but at the moment, they vanish. Like a roaring sea has ripped through my head, washing away its contents and leaving nothing but chaos in its wake.

"You're new here, right?" The man creeps out towards me from the shadows with a small smile on his face. He looks younger than I'd thought. I eye him wearily but nod my response, stepping back from him to maintain my distance. His dark eyes shine, a glint of something I don't trust. I may be young, but I still trust my instincts on this.

"It's okay. I work here. Come closer and let me get a look at you."

I don't want him to look. In fact, I want to run again. His eyes and hair are both impossibly black, blending him into the surrounding darkness. I don't care if he works here or not; I don't want any answers from this man.

This man screams violence.

Pain.

Hunger.

"Come now, I won't hurt you. Not really. In fact, you might enjoy what I've got planned."

Bile rises. I've heard of the birds and the bees. Pretty sure every twelve-year-old has had some sort of fantasy, but what this man is insinuating, I will not be enjoying one bit. My pulse pounds in an erratic beat as anxiety completely takes over. My body freezes.

"You're a pretty little thing, aren't you?" The man circles me, inching ever closer as I try to move away. I'm a fly caught in a web I've unknowingly run straight into.

The other boy had been right to warn me.

I shudder as this man's stare invades my body on an uncomfortable level. My sodden pyjamas cling to my skin, not shrouding me from his inspection. I know what's coming, know I'm too small and too weak to fight him, and that I'm too exhausted to run. The determination is radiating off him in waves, his muscular frame intimidating with each stalking step he takes.

Warmth trails down my leg as the panic fully takes control, my breathing harsh and uneven. I'm like a deer in headlights—unable to move. The man slowly sniffs with a feral grin. I don't understand how he can smell me from where he is.

"Aw, how precious. You pissed yourself. That's alright. I don't mind it being a little bit dirty as long as it's rough. Here, let me show you," he sneers, licking his lips.

He prowls forward, and I still can't find it in myself to move. My mind is screaming at me to run, to fight, but I'm stock still. Why can't I move? His hand grips the back of my neck tightly, and I gasp in pain as he manoeuvres a leg in front of mine. His leg trips me to the floor and I land painfully on my knees.

Forcefully, he pushes my face into the mud. The bitter taste of dirt fills my mouth as I try to scream in protest.

As his body climbs over mine, I start that impossible fight to escape. It's like a switch; my body finally catches up with my mind. The storm rages above, uncaring as I twist and writhe, trying to escape his grasp to no avail. As I buck, I feel the hardness of him digging into my backside, and I squeak out my fright.

"That's it. Fight me, little one. You seem to know exactly what I want from you," he groans, grinding his erection against me. This time, I am sick. Right into the mud in front of me.

He laughs coldly. Like a naughty dog, he thrusts my nose into my vomit. He removes most of his weight from my back while keeping a firm hand on my neck to keep me in place. He's trapped my hands beneath my body, and I can do nothing as he shoves my PJ bottoms down to my ankles. I whimper as he shifts my knees through the slick mud beneath me, pushing my arse into the air while my head is to the ground. Briefly, the motion frees my hands and I try to use my new position to gain purchase to run, but he's too fast. He grips my wrists and roughly tugs them together behind my back. Holding them with one of his own, he shoves me forward once more.

"That's it, you little bitch." The stinging crack of his palm on my behind brings tears to my eyes. The hopelessness of the situation overcomes me, and I try to shut down what's happening as his hand assaults me over and over. His words become a tirade of madness that I don't want to invade my mind. Rain drips down my hair, my lashes, and my cheeks. I try to concentrate on everything surrounding me and not on my reality. Trees watch on and a buzz of insects call out in the night in this hellish world I'm now a part of.

A shadow lurks in the periphery of my vision, watching my humiliating position. As the shape moves forward, I recognise the boy I ran from earlier—the one who offered to help me. I should have listened to him instead of running, but he's older, and my scared brain couldn't fathom that he would actually help me.

The zipper is like a shotgun in the night, silencing everything in the surrounding area. My eyes widen. I look up in terrified horror to seek out the boy. I pray he will still want to save me, but I can no longer see him.

"Let him go," the teen's voice speaks out.

A dull thud sounds before the hand gripping me releases my wrists. The weight over my body moves and I scramble away, tripping slightly on the pyjamas wrapped around my ankles. But I don't care; I just rush to my saviour, hiding behind him, like a child behind their mother's skirts. Then, and only then, do I pull them up to cover myself. I look back to where I'd come from and catch sight of the rock on the floor. Blood is now pouring from my tormentor's head. Should we run? Would he come after us?

The older boy glares at the man as he stands strong over him. My mind whirls. His chest heaves with an agitated noise as he looks over his wide shoulder at me. I look down at my feet, wriggling my toes inside my socks. I didn't mean to make him mad.

"You little shit, you'll pay for that. He needs his injection," the man spits out venomously. What injection? Hasn't he done enough to me? "In fact, you need yours. Come here willingly, the pair of you, and for tonight, I'll leave this be."

I don't understand. Nothing in this place makes any sense. My stomach whirls, and my body shakes with confusion and shock. I look up at the boy through my eyelashes, wondering if we could just go. He fingers something inside his pocket and looks thoughtful at the request. After a moment, he nods and pulls out a stone dagger.

"Whatever helps you sleep at night, princess. You may have gotten me once with that thing, but I'm ready for it next time."

The man examines something on the watch I hadn't noticed before. I can't see what it says. Everything here is so strange. It's like this is normal. He pulls out a black zipped case from his jacket pocket and takes out two needles. He fills them both with different coloured liquids. I dare not ask what is inside these concoctions.

The boy holds his hand out to me. I look at his outstretched palm for only a second before gripping it tightly in mine. He saved me once; I just hope I can trust him as we walk back to the man who assaulted me. In front of the man, he lets my hand go to have the needle jabbed roughly into his neck. I wince before taking my place. The man places an arm around my waist, giving me a leering look with his penetrating black eyes.

"I had fun tonight. Shame we were interrupted. Next time, maybe I'll be luckier. I don't enjoy an audience as much as others." His quiet words make me shudder. He injects me in the neck, and it isn't as painful as I expected. However, the pat on the butt as I turn away makes me want to puke again.

I can't stop the tears that trail down my cheeks when my saviour grabs my hand, dragging me quickly away as I shake more violently. My wobbly legs have me stumbling through the woods as I follow him. Glad for his reassuring presence to guide me, I remember that I don't even know his name.

"Thank you. I'm Dario." My throat is so closed up, sobs desperate to escape that I can't say anything else. Wouldn't even know what to say. I shouldn't have run, I should have stayed with him, listened to him. I was stupid. Those things are all painfully obvious and do not need to be said. I'm disgusted with myself for freezing like I did. If I hadn't frozen, perhaps I could've gotten away.

"Huck," he coughs slightly, then contemplates me, still leading the way. "You're lucky you ran in this direction, and I didn't go too far. I heard you cry out. I wish you'd listened to me. That one is one of the worst. He's insane. The others mostly just inject and take off, but not him. I've seen him leave boys for dead after he's through with them," he says. A shudder radiates through our joined hands, making me incredibly grateful for his intervention. "Come on, the cave is just through here."

Huck leads me through the trees to a secluded spot

where a crop of vast rocks are jutting from the earth. Each seems to be sitting on top of the other in a crude sort of tower, held together by time, weight, and the nature surrounding it. They dip and flow, leaving small gaps which I can only assume are the caves Huck is leading us towards.

"A few guys and the youngsters use this cave system to bed down in. We try to look out for each other a bit, but we have caves to ourselves. I sleep just a little way up, if you're okay to climb while it's slippery. I have a stash of food, water, and a change of clothes for now until we can get to the outpost," he explains. At my nod, he releases my hand. I find I miss the comfort of his secure grip, but I understand why as he grabs hold of the stones.

In the rocks are indents, corrosion over time perhaps, but more likely carved out with tools. Huck was right, clambering the ladder like foot holds in the rain is slippery and slow going, especially with so little light. My hands are practically frozen, my feet are hardly any better, and my legs are still trembling as Huck once again holds his hand out to me. Pulling me up the last of the way, I stumble into him. Huck wraps his arms around me to hold me steady. I look up at him while my face heats as I try to pull away. He just grins and his face brightens as he keeps me held firm but gently in his arms. It's so warm.

"It's all good. Don't be embarrassed. I'm not going to hurt you," he whispers softly, tucking a strand of my soaked hair behind my ear. "You're so skittish, Dario. I'm gonna need to toughen you up a little bit, huh? Now, come on, this way," he croons. A soft smile plays on my lips as I duck my head and realise just how nice older boys can be. Or, at least, this one is.

He leads me towards one of the cave openings with an arm wrapped around my waist. I'm aware of just how filthy I am right now, covered in rain, mud, and my piss, and my smile turns to embarrassment as the acrid smell hits me. I think about how pathetic I am, what I must look like to him. How can this older boy want to help me? Be kind to me? Let alone touch me? Step after step, I follow his lead, feeling all the worse. I will myself not to break down into a sobbing mess like I had been when I'd met him, pushing myself to be stronger, braver.

We walk into the mouth of the cave and follow the tunnel. There's little light. The only exception is the dappled light from the moon shimmering through the trees. The deeper we delve, the darker into the abyss we go. I have no idea how Huck knows where we're going because I can see nothing at all. After a time, he stops and moves away from me when we get about a hundred feet inside. Clawing fear unfurls inside me at being alone in the unending dark. Noises sound out in the surrounding area making me jump. There's a hiss, a crackle, and then flames spring from a match to my right. Huck lights a sconce on the wall.

"Home, sweet home."

I blink at the sudden brightness invading my vision to remove the dots now spotting my sight. As things begin to clear, I take in the cavern, seeing the many plastic boxes and bags littered to one side and a fire pit in the middle. Looking up, I notice it's the perfect spot to shelter—little crevasses in the cave roof allowing the curling smoke to leave but stops the rain from pouring through. I ponder if this was yet more man-made workmanship or just another of nature's wonders.

Huck crouches to the boxes. He unclips one of them and sorts through. He sets things beside him, reseals the box, and methodically moves to the next. Clothes, tins and a canteen appear, along with a saucepan and what looks to be some wood shavings. Next to the boxes he opens a bag to reveal wood of different shapes and sizes. Huck proceeds to drag his findings over to the fire pit.

"How did you know we'd made it here? It's so dark," curiosity laces my voice. I watch as Huck pats his pocket and pulls out the matches he had used to light the sconce on the wall. He turns and puts them carefully back inside a box while considering his answer.

"Echoes of our footfalls. Once you hit the cavern, they change sound. Plus, I've done this like a million times. I used to use a torch to get through, but it's been so long I didn't even think to," he says. He seems sheepish about admitting it, but really, I'm more fascinated than upset. "I've been here maybe five years now. Not sure. I was ten when I was taken. I think I'm fifteen now." Huck shrugs nonchalantly, but the sadness in his eyes tells a different story.

I wonder if he's lonely? If that's why he stood up to a full-grown man to help me? The fact he's been here so long is disturbing; it means any hope I may have of getting home is well and truly gone in my mind.

"Oh."

My only response. It's stupid. Childish. But really, what more could I say? "Can I help you with anything?"

Huck smiles as he hands me a small bundle of clothes and returns to the logs in the bag.

Fascinated, I watch as he places the wood shavings down first, then stacks a small, almost tepee shaped pile of sticks over them. I'm so mesmerised by the process, I forget the clothes in my arms. I can't look away as he stands, grabbing the sconce on the wall to light the kindling in multiple places before putting it back in place. As the fire appears to grow, he slowly adds wood to the fire, starting with the smaller logs, then going up in size until the warmth from the flames filters through my body.

A wracking cough takes over Huck, and I give him a worried look. He bends over away from the blaze and his chest rattles. I drop the clothes and hurry across the room, finding the canteen where he'd left it. I shake it and am relieved to hear the liquid sploshing inside. Opening it, I hand it to Huck, hoping a drink may help ease him. A few sips and his breathing eases, his cough dying down.

"Thanks. Think I got a lungful of smoke there. Teach me to show off when I saw you watching," he laughs before taking another small sip of water. "We really need to get out of these wet clothes. Tomorrow, maybe we'll get a wash down at the bay on the way to the outpost. Since you're here, I'm guessing that'll be restocked with new things."

"What's the outpost?" I hadn't asked before, but if we were going tomorrow, it's best I know what I'm getting myself in to. Walking back to my borrowed clothes, I pull off my wet top, but pause as I go to take off the pyjama pants. I turn my back on Huck as I sense my body go beet red. It's not like I've never shared a changing room with the boys at school before, but this feels somehow different.

"It's like a shop, I suppose, but instead of paying, you take what you need to survive. If you try to take more than you need... Well, let's just say, don't ever try to take more than you need."

"Why?" I turn back to him now, fully dressed in black sweats and a tee, sporting a pair of fluffy socks. It appears Huck doesn't own any shoes. In the time I'd turned around, Huck had taken the time to clothe himself too. Fluffy socks and all.

"It's a death sentence," he says, looking at me gravely, any sense of the joking and laughter gone. I swallow and nod.

"Come on, I'll make us something to eat. Soup okay? And here, have a drink," Huck continues as he passes me the canteen and gets to work, emptying the tins out into the saucepan without waiting for my response.

Time passes quickly, with overall lighter conversation, jokes and smiles from him. Questions and maddening anxiousness from me. Throughout the evening, our talking comes to sudden stops as another coughing fit starts up for Huck, who immediately blames the smoke. Eventually, he concedes, confirming the suspicion I have that something is wrong.

"Shit, this jab is going to be bad. It might be a virus or something. I'm exhausted all of a sudden," Huck yawns out, his body violently shivering, his arms raising in goosebumps, his forehead shiny with sweat. "It's so cold," he says, teeth chattering.

Quickly, I scout the boxes in the cave, finding a blanket, sleeping bag, and pillow.

"Is this something they normally give out? Will you be okay? I don't think there's anything wrong with me. I can't have been given the same thing, so maybe I can watch over you?" My words are a jumbled mess as I set up the sleeping bag and pillow as close to the fire as safely as possible. He settles inside and I drape the blanket over the top of him for extra warmth, my eyes searching, wondering if there's anything else I can do for him.

"I've had it before, so it shouldn't be so bad this time, antibodies or whatever. Maybe your jab was a dud. It happens sometimes. You'll get used to it. I just need to rest. I'd really love it if you played nurse maid though," his teasing voice makes my heart lighter.

I rest my hand on his clammy forehead. His head is scalding hot, and I bite my lip to evade the worry. It doesn't work, but I vow nothing will happen to the boy who has saved me.

"Sweet dreams. I'll look after you," I breathe out. He gives me a sleepy smile in thanks and his eyes drift shut.

In the glowing firelight, I watch the steady rise and fall of Huck's chest as he sleeps. For the first time since I came to this place, I experience something akin to safety. This boy has protected me from a nightmare I never could've ever imagined before; now it is my time to look after him. He said the injection was normal here, something I'd become used to. I'm not so sure about that.

Pulling my sleeping bag right next to Huck was purely a decision made to keep tabs on him throughout the night. Resting my head on his chest so I can listen to the steady thump of his heart, however, was something I couldn't explain even to myself. One thing I knew for certain was that things were never going to be the same again.

CHAPTER 4

HUCK

Age Fifteen

My skin burns.

I feel the volcanic heat from within. It has me wanting to claw at my scorching skin, to shed off a layer to cool down my insides. I know logically it's just a virus, a symptom of whatever torrid poison the hunters of the night have given me, but I'm so fucking hot. I may as well be in the fires of hell themselves.

I try to raise my hands, to scratch at my neck, but find my arms pinned down at my side. Groaning, I squint my eyes open, I hadn't even realised they were still shut. The campfire is too bright in my dark cave; the light hurting my sensitive eyes as it flickers across the walls. I wonder how long I have slept.

"Huck, are you okay?" The voice pulls me from my musings. A delicate hand touches my blanket-covered chest and I frown. I never use these blankets. Looking up, I find the worried freckled face of a young boy. I watch wearily as he pulls at the blankets, trying to pull them higher over my sweat-covered shoulders.

I choose not to answer. Instead, I follow his movements as he potters around the cave, going through my boxes of supplies and gathering what I think might be dinner. Enough for the two of us. My water canteen in hand, he walks back over to me, offering it out to me as if it were his to give. Is the water inside even boiled? I doubt a child could possibly know to do that.

"Do you need anything?" he asks me as I stare at him, his pure green eyes staring right back.

"Who the fuck are you?" I whisper. I don't really know if I'm speaking the question to myself or to him. Either way, the words are probably harsher than they need to be. I'm confused and I don't like that someone has encroached on my space without permission, but as I take in the boy's hurt face, a flicker of guilt fills me.

He's just a kid.

It's been a long time since I felt like I could be just a kid. Even before this place, my mum and dad didn't have much time for me anymore. Not after my big brother died. It was like, after he passed on, the world stopped existing. Left to my own devices, I had to look after myself from a young age.

"I'm Dario. Sorry, I didn't mean to be a bother. I'll go," he croaks before he flees. Running into the pitch-black tunnel leading to freedom. My heart sinks, instant remorse at letting this boy go out to the wilderness on his own. I can't let him get hurt.

"No, kid, wait!" My words are wasted, his echoing footfalls dimming as he gets further away. I strain against the blankets but find I'm too weak to move. My canteen sits tauntingly close by, and I'm desperate for just a drop, the heat of my body having parched my throat.

I battle and wriggle, trying to release just one arm from my blanketed cocoon. The struggle heats my body further, exhausting my already tired limbs. I still, closing my weary eyes for just a moment. I just need to let myself rest enough to gain the energy to escape this heated death trap.

Footsteps close by startle me and I curse, realising I must have dozed off, but that doesn't matter. The kid, Dario, must have returned, and I'd rather be awake to greet him. I'm groggy, and know I couldn't have been asleep for long, but I want to make sure the first thing I say to him is genuine.

"Shit, kid, I'm glad you're back. I'm so—" my words are cut off.

"It's just me," a familiar voice calls. Peter steps into the light, his flop of blonde hair hangs over his eyes like usual. He smiles as he walks over to me. "The kid said you might need some water before he ran off. Said it had been a little while, and he was worried. Seemed like a good guy. Shame you scared him off. He was doing a good job looking after you."

Only a few months older than me, Peter came to the island around about the same time I had. We couldn't be more different though. Where he found himself more involved in the camp, I preferred to help with the more individual tasks. I liked to keep watch or scout out new sources of food and water. Then I'd volunteer to trek to the outpost alone when we needed minimal supplies. He is more interested in dealing with the disputes and niggles of day-to-day camp life.

I preferred the aspects I can keep control of; you can't control people.

"He wasn't looking after me. He was smothering me. I'm boiling. Let me out of here, will you?"

Peter barks out a laugh, moving forward to free me from the prison of blankets. He sits me up and passes me my flask. I inspect the water, wondering if it's clean enough to drink. To hell with it, I tip it to my lips, my desperation apparent as it quenches my thirst.

"You know that shy little thing came and asked me what to do when he thought you would die. You've been out of it for days. You were shivering, you know. You needed the heat. Kid even checked where to get your replacement water. As you're already drinking it, you should be damn grateful he found out how to sanitise it too."

I'm shocked. That small, innocent looking creature did all that for me. I don't think I've ever had someone do anything like that for me before. I keep my eyes on my hands, scratching the dirt from underneath my fingernails. The gnawing guilt sinks deep inside my gut, chewing me from the inside.

Now he's out there all alone, because of me, when all he was trying to do was help.

"You do remember being the one to bring him back, right? I mean, we were all pretty damn shocked when you rocked up with him, but the way you're acting right now is like he's an uninvited intruder."

"He wasn't. I mean, I appreciate what he did, but..."

"Huck, I don't know what to tell you except you brought him back to your cave," Peter interrupts me, his voice stern. So unlike his usual jovial tone that normally grates on my nerves. My stomach is in pieces, chewed up, spat out, and clawing guiltily at my insides.

"Shit, really? I honestly had no idea. Do you know where he went?"

"When I realised he was leaving, I tracked him a couple of miles away. When he saw me, he bolted. There was no way I could keep up with him. Ironically, the only person with that kind of stamina is you," Peter replies, passing me some dried meat, an apple, and a protein bar.

"Eat up, then shift out. You've got a kid to find."

Two days and I've only caught brief glimpses of him. From what I have learned from Peter, there is only one more day until the sirens ring. My gut churns at the thought of Dario being out here when that time comes. Pressure makes my head ache, an unyielding tension I won't be able to ease until I find him.

I fear the things I may have forgotten. Not liking the thought of what harm could be caused by the gaps in my memory. Placing a hand over my pocket, I pat the familiar outline, checking my knife is in place. Sturdy and safe, exactly where it should be. I breathe out a small sigh of relief at its reassuring presence. At least in that one thing I can be certain of.

As the hours go by, I wonder if I'll ever be able to bring him back home as I trek through the woods on this island. I've avoided the more frequented areas so far, but soon I'll have to change my trajectory.

Stopping for a break, I pull the canteen from my pack and take a swig of water. The rustle of movement up ahead has me putting the flask away, careful to make no sound. Keeping my eyes peeled for danger, I crouch low in the dense greenery. I know full well just because the sirens haven't sounded doesn't mean all the danger is gone. Half the men on this island are just as deadly. Another reason to bring Dario safely back with me.

I spot someone running full pelt towards me in the distance. They don't spot me, their focus purely on the momentum of their stride. I duck further into the bush; they might be escaping from a more lethal threat I need to avoid.

As they move steadily closer, I notice it's the figure of a boy, one with curls of red hair. A smirk crosses my features at this minor stroke of luck. Here I was, thinking I was about to be dealing with someone more threatening than me, but here comes my own prey instead.

As he approaches, I ready myself, waiting for the perfect moment to pounce. I leap out from the bush, and he lets out a startled screech, falling backwards harshly onto his behind. I can't help the chuckle I let out, holding out my hand to help him up.

I watch with interest when he looks like he's going to refuse. There's a desperate urge to resist my help, but he begrudgingly gives in. I pull Dario to his feet, hand soft in my calloused palm. He stumbles over his own feet, and I put my arms around his waist to steady him. His face heats red, and he forcefully pushes away from me, turning to race away once again.

My mind sparks with recognition. I'd almost left him after his first rejection but that scream and seeing his scared face so desperate and alone. His pleading eyes begging me for help as a black-eyed predator took him to the floor.

His small hand clinging tightly to my own, his innocence shining through. I couldn't help but take Dario under my wing, I couldn't let anyone take advantage of him. I just can't remember why I'd allowed him into my space when there had been so many others to spare. Maybe I hadn't considered past that first night. I'd just figured he was my responsibility, and I had just wanted to give him a safe place to stay. I don't know, but I what I do know is I can't let him get away from me now.

I need to protect him.

"Dario!" I call out as he flees. I chase after him, never allowing him to get out of my view. The sun has been hotter the past couple of days, making the mud firm beneath my feet. It gives me a better advantage in this chase as most people from before never truly run barefoot on the hardened, cracked mud of the earth like we do here.

As foliage whips past me, catching at my clothes and skin, I don't let it slow my pace. Keeping my eyes firmly on my target, I follow him onwards. Peter was right, his stamina is outstanding. At a guess, he's had no problems finding food and water since he left the caves either. His body is by no means weakened by dehydration or lack of nutrients.

Tenacious little thing. A little fighter, with a true inner strength, despite his more nervous quirks.

"You're so skittish, Dario. I'm gonna need to toughen you up a little bit, huh?"

My own words resonate through my mind as I picture

his blushing face peering up at me. His green gaze held an unquestioning faith in my ability to look after him. I had held him tight, knowing that it was the right thing to do. That he had needed me to make him stronger as I pushed back a lock of his red hair.

That moment in the rain, I had made my decision.

I knew his life had become mine to keep safe. He had needed me, and I had let him down. It was unforgivable, but I would have to gain his trust back once more.

I keep my pursuit of him swift and agile, never faltering as I move through the thickening bramble of thorny shrubs. Determination pushes me onward as I hear his little startled yelps of pain. I know the pricks of discomfort from the thorns are causing this sweet boy much more bother than they are to me.

He comes to a stop, surrounded by towering vines covered in spindly bristles. With nowhere to go, and I slow, edging ever closer. He spins, eyes widening as he sees me.

"I'm so sorry, Dario. I didn't remember."

Like the proverbial lion with a thorn in its paw, Dario whimpers, backing away further from me. I can't blame him. I raise my hands, trying to ease his fear. His eyes flick behind me and around the enclosed space. Seeing he has no escape, he deflates, defeated. I hate that look in his eyes and almost want to give him the space to run once more. I can't; won't do that.

"Dario, I need you to listen to me," I try to ease him with soft words. His green eyes glance up at mine before looking back down at his muddy feet. I sigh. "Dario, the injection that man gave me made me really sick, right?" I continue, willing him to understand. His eyes still down, he nods his reply.

"You helped me through that, and I'm so incredibly grateful to you. What I need you to understand is when I first woke up. When I first saw you again..." I say, looking away from him. The words are almost too hard to speak as I go over what it had cost him to trust me after what he had been through. Only to have it thrown back in his face. As I look back at Dario, his green eyes are back on mine. Watching me intently and I realise I only have this one chance to make things right.

"When I first saw you again, I thought you were a stranger. Of all the mental things, I thought it was you taking advantage of me, stealing my belongings and maybe even trying to kill me. It's so stupid, but I didn't remember you. Whatever the drugs did to me, it was more than just the virus. Hell, maybe the virus made me insane. Either way, I'm just so sorry."

I close my eyes and sigh, my hand going to the back of my head, mussing my hair up in agitation. I'm so out of sorts right now. Unable to process the deep-seated irrational anger and loathing for my unwarranted behaviour. Yet, I'm so desperate for his forgiveness.

Rationally, I know it hadn't been my fault. I need him to know it wasn't my fault and I hope that I have shown that it is not my usual behaviour. Not that he makes me act so normally, bringing out that protective instinct inside of me.

I feel so different.

So unlike myself that when his laughter breaks out, I don't know if I should laugh right along with his crazy arse or bawl my eyes out. Does he feel that way too?

I choose to laugh.

CHAPTER 5

NIXI

Age Twelve

I know what is happening to me, yet I don't know if I am really here at all. I can feel the violation of my body with each unwanted thrust. The screams of my own agony echoes around, but as I float above myself, watching this happen to me, I start to wonder.

Is that even me?

I stare down at the scene in disbelief. There is a connection between my body below and my current spirit-like state, but I'm confused. I don't understand. Two separate entities, but just one in control. Fractured. Mind fighting and body frozen, I try to get my body to fight back against the man who lies atop of me, but I can't. Weak swipes of my hands are not enough to do a thing, my legs remaining paralysed in the dry dirt beneath me.

It has only been minutes since the siren's shrill tone stopped. This man pounced quickly. His body is so much larger than my own; easily overcoming my small stature. It didn't take long for my screams to sound along with the other women's as I struggled.

I feel dirty, used, and degraded as he pins me down with his crushing weight by the dying glow of the campfire. He roughly fondles and tweaks my breasts through the dirty white material of my dress. Moving his large, calloused hands roughly across my bare hips and arse, lifting the hem of my dress without care for my dignity. My body is his plaything for the night. He cares nothing for my happiness and enjoys painting my skin with bruising marks.

As I beg and plead pitifully, asking for mercy, he laughs. This black-eyed demon only takes pleasure in my misery. His laughter scares me, and I cower further into the mud, twisting my head away from this beast. I'm weak, helpless and completely powerless. Not even my bitten nails scratching into him can do any damage as he howls his enjoyment into the night sky.

I don't know if my mind has become disjointed. I'm looking away, but I can still observe from above, still witness each thrusting movement of his body as he pushes inside of mine. Is this a dream or perhaps my trauma's messed up way of protecting my mind?

Or maybe it has something to do with the needle he plunged into my neck moments before he pushed me down. Am I just high right now? There were a couple of older foster kids' back home that were always out of their heads on something.

I am both here and there; I don't know which is worse. I close my eyes; two pairs close, one physical set and one phantom. I am mildly more orientated, but it doesn't stop the fear of what is happening to me as he takes away my innocence.

Gripping my hair tightly in his fist, he lifts me painfully upwards, changing the angle of his penetrations. Hitting a spot deeper within me, I shriek out a painful cry, my head flinging back, shock ripping strands of my hair from my scalp.

Tears dampen my cheeks and the wet lick of his tongue slides over my skin, consuming my misery. I scrunch my eyes closed even tighter, unwilling to watch the monster both above me and below me. Unable to let myself witness his satisfaction as he takes more from me.

He's barely a man, an older teenager perhaps, but that doesn't sway his cruelties as his hips slap harder against me. I don't understand what could make him think this is right. Shadows of men in the darkness creep into our rundown shacks, followed by the screams of the girls.

As he ruts into me like an animal possessed, there's a snap within me. My being zaps wholly above, as my physical body can no longer take the punishing force it's being made to take.

Is this death?

Suddenly, I open my eyes, I have to know. I turn over my noncorporeal hands and shudder at the ability to view straight through the other side. Have I become a ghost to this horror show? I glide closer to my physical form; my eyes may be closed, but it seems I am still breathing. My chest slowly rises and falls.

For now, at least.

The connection to my body and its pain is now broken. A blissful reprieve from the torturous hurt this man is bestowing upon me as he rips away my virginity. In a not-so-distant memory, learning about sex, me and my best friend Zee giggled, both swearing we would wait until we found Mr Right. Guess that option is no longer mine to choose. At least someone has not brought her here. She's not suffering this same futile destiny.

Curling up next to my body, I take a slight comfort in watching my chest rise and fall. Reassured that despite the lacking connection, I am still alive. I don't know what has happened to me, or how, but I still draw breath.

This monster of a man can't see me, making no reaction to my presence in this form. I touch a hand to my physical shoulder, but it goes straight through. I don't know what I expected, maybe to merge back together with myself. Like I had seen in that movie, the one I was too young to see, heck I probably still am. But for now, at least, I am stuck apart.

The girls' screams have died down, much like my own. All that's left are a few echoing whimpers. I wonder how those that ran have fared? Did they escape this act of violence or is fleeing just a futile attempt to prolong the inevitable? They knew enough to run. I've been on this island for a week, and no one told me what to do or what was coming.

Fliss has abandoned me.

Hurt thrums through my translucent veins at the thought of how the door was so unforgivingly flung in my face. She had known what the sirens brought. What these men would do to me, yet she offered me no reassurances, no comforts, only her brutal betrayal.

I turn over, putting my back to the scene, not able to look any longer as the monstrous man violates my body. His grunting crescendo of moaning pleasure is something I long to mute. I stare out into the darkness of the camp. I can only make out the faint glow of coals from fires burning out, barely there, until they're snuffed out into ashes.

A door bangs, and my head swings in that direction. I squint my eyes, trying to make out the looming shadow that makes its way out from Fliss's home. I move forward, my ghostly form floating easily above the camp.

My eyes widen in shock as I draw close. Fliss's limp

body is slung over the shoulder of another man. Her silvery, hovering form trailing close behind him as he walks them away from camp. Not once does she glance in my direction, but as she drifts past my broken body, I swear there's a look of guilt on her face. Especially when she ignores me as I call her name.

AGE THIRTEEN

I close my eyes with the sound of the siren, shoulders hunched, and take in slow, deep breaths. Chris's hand squeezes my shoulder as she rises from our seated position by my fire. The older girl isn't a friend, not exactly, but she is the only company I have on this island. Especially since Fliss disappeared.

I hadn't known as her translucent hovering form had followed her physically unconscious body that it would be the last time I would see her. How could I have known that? But I know the others blame me for her being taken. I don't know why though; it's not like I could have stopped it, even if I tried. As I am pushed further and further outside of the group, I know they place me solely at fault.

Chris went against the grain; she dislikes the mentality

of the group. She has never been a leader like Fliss, always sticking to herself, following the rules and keeping her head down. I know she only stays with me out of pity, not a genuine appreciation for me. For her, I'm the lesser of two evils. I accept it, and it beats the silence. Plus, I quite like the sarcastic older teen and hope one day she'll grow to return the favour.

I open my eyes and watch Chris's progress as she runs along the pathway towards the beach; the wind pulling at her roughly shorn hair. I still have time to run, or time to hide, but I have yet to decide this week's game plan.

It is a game I am tired of playing. The same repetition of that shrill call signalling you to make your move. To decide where you want to be on the board of their chess game, with them always ten steps ahead.

I don't know exactly how long I've been on this island, but it must be around a year. A year of torment and harrowing experiences I can't bear to relive. From my body being violated time and time again by multiple different men, to the stinging pinch of a needle with an unknown surprise to be had.

Over that time, I have learned things, taken in the knowledge of how these men work, to use that to my advantage. The problem is, I am growing so tired of playing. I am sick of the certain result and numb to the pain of their victory.

Am I truly willing to give up the fight?

Each of these predators has a preference. The first kind lives on the thrill of their victims staying hidden in the shadows of the rundown homes we live in. Breathing in our fright as they stand inside our doorways, watching us and waiting. They let the fear ratchet up inside us, enjoying our inability to escape. They wait for every anxious-riddled pore to fill, and when we are just about ready to break, they make their move.

These are the monsters who like to creep under our beds at night. Knowing each time they come to our door, the memory will come to haunt us. The fear of their presence re-emerging in the dead of the night has some girls huddled together. No longer able to sleep alone; no longer willing to use their own beds. I can't blame them.

I have no option but to remain alone.

The second kind of predator lives for the hunt, the chase, and the catch. Stalking their prey through the forested landscape of the island. These beasts are the least complicated of the three types of predators that keep us trapped here.

That perhaps makes them the most confusing of all.

They can cause us harm in the pursuit without remorse and happily inject us with unknown substances. Strangely, it is rare for them to use us for their pleasure and, from what Chris told me, on those rare occasions, it has never been with the younger girls. The hunt satisfies their real wants and needs.

The third kind is the worst predator of them all; one who lives for the pain. These demons don't care which way they achieve their goal, as long as it hurts. It doesn't matter how old their prey is, they will always end up being left weak and vulnerable where they lie. Sometimes even left for dead.

These are the men I try to avoid as the siren rings, as they hunt me relentlessly across the island. I hadn't known what was going on; not known what was coming for me the first time. When the black-eyed devil had taken his fill, he merely laughed. Enjoying my fruitless fight as I barely scratched at his skin.

Now, he's set his friends—the ones who enjoy the pain —the task of ruining me further. I don't know if it's better to stay and face the monsters in my home or go out and risk the demons. I don't have much time left to decide. The siren has been ringing for a while now, and the silence will signal their start.

Either way, I am caught, and when it happens, it is guaranteed to hurt.

Aggs had decided against telling me about the siren. It had been her job back in the warehouse that first day. I've not confronted the woman about it, or what she said about me down on the beach. Is it worth it with all the trauma we go through?

No new girls have arrived since me, and I have a sinking suspicion that the decision is not down to the men currently waiting in the treeline. Not that I would ever speak those thoughts aloud. Thoughts of the women who took away my choice makes my anger flare. She had no empathy, no kindness inside her dark heart.

I could not move in so much terror as he ripped away my virtue. If they had given me any kind of knowledge, I could've at least known not to bother fighting back against a psycho like him. He needs to see the fear and pain, wants to witness the fish struggling on the end of his line. I could have saved my energy.

Though, more likely, I would've run, just like I do now.

I can't give up yet.

CHAPTER 6

RAFFERTY

Age Ten

It's been a strange few months.

Although Aiden's recovery has been smoother than I could have imagined, he will never fully be free from the dull ache constantly throbbing in his arm. His gold eyes holding a pain no one our age should have to understand. We leave his latest appointment with no further relief, only more disappointment.

Closing the metal door of the medical wing behind us, I stand by him. Keeping him safe from the feral vibes my brothers give off. Moving through our dungeon home, we ignore the smug smiles and whispered words of lounging boys. Knowing that interacting will only bring more pain.

I make sure Aiden stays standing tall, even when he doesn't think he can. The fluorescent light shining back off the white walls is too bright for how we are both feeling. Our mood is much more suited to the darkness, but we are given no choice but to be bathed in this endless light.

Walking through the first common area of our underground home is a tactical assessment. With so many brothers, it becomes a matter of importance to avoid the majority, not wanting to earn their wrath and have it become problematic.

We already know to steer clear of Devon and his closest accomplices in the gym, a spot known to all of us. The only time when they venture elsewhere is for meals, games, or curfew. The rest of our brothers prefer to spread out across various rooms within our living quarters. Walking through the lounge room gives us an idea of how widespread they are. With so many rooms, it is impossible to avoid everyone.

The quickest option would be to bypass all common areas to our dorms through the main corridor. It's not for the faint of heart though. If trapped and surrounded there by multiple brothers on the hunt, you're in for a world of hurt. Two of my brothers fell to Devon's violence this way, surrounded by his most faithful cronies.

It's why careful calculation and probability are so

essential; to find the safest route to our dorm in peace. The daily task of mapping our home is an endless chore; a challenge we shouldn't have to deal with. A necessary evil to keep us alive.

The laughter behind us still does not grant me the answer we need to know. I look at Aiden, quirking my eyebrow in question. Ahead to the canteen, or right into the main walkway. We both know better than to go into Devon's territory.

I watch as his eyes close briefly, brow creasing in concentration as his lips move his unspoken thoughts. Opening his eyes, he indicates the corridor with his hand, and I smile, nodding as we move onward. After all, he taught me the probabilities and I trust his instincts. His only mistake—resulting in his current injuries—thankfully didn't cost him his life. With such a high price to pay, Aiden had still had luck on his side with me so close by to bind his arm.

A risk he will not take again.

We live on Venatio: an island made up of human lab rats. Like vermin in the sewers, me and my brothers reside below the main facility. Watched over mostly by one doctor. His goal in keeping us is unclear, but it's obvious he has no intention of letting us escape to a world outside of this one.

I know he is doing something to us. It's clear in the way he studies us. Writing his notes on each of us, pitting us against one another. I don't like to be used, but to him —to the man who ultimately raised me—I am nothing but a game piece for him to manipulate. To tamper with and control until I do as he deems worthy. It's endlessly testing my frustrations, especially as I watch him plot his next strategy.

Now, one by one, my brothers are changing. They differ from how they once were. We have always been on the darker side. Have always fought and played our games, but now they seem to crave the violence. A need as potent as food and water. A far more sadistic way of life since the brothers following in Devon's footsteps grows in number.

It hadn't been Devon who flung Aiden from the tree that night. It hadn't just been Aiden that was injured. My brothers prey on the younger of us, the ones who they deem the weakest, like me and Aiden.

The ones who lose the trials.

I've asked questions to those I know are less likely to instigate brutality. I am desperate for the truth of what makes them this way. None of them will talk about it. They all give each other knowing looks as if they're in on some big secret. Are they actually in on it though, or is something happening to them without their under-standing?

Whatever is happening to our brothers, I need to find out.

Devon's strength and speed seems to grow as each day passes and he's not the only one. I watch as many of my brothers run circles around me and Aiden. We can no longer keep up with them, no matter how much we try. If we try to fight back, or more likely, I try to; they beat us down into submission.

Aiden's look of defeat has me nudging his elbow, reminding him to keep his chin held high. He knows better than any other that to be seen as weak is akin to a death sentence. His nod reassures my pounding heart. We lost another brother only days ago to the bloodshed of Devon's making.

I won't lose Aiden too.

I've discussed it with Aiden at length. Neither of us can understand what is making them capable of the things they do. The nurses who care for me and my brothers pay Devon extra attention now. The doctor calls for him more often. He's not the eldest here, but he has a quality, it seems, that has everyone bowing to his whims.

Devon, the leader of this band of deviants, laps up the devotion given to him by his sycophants, simpering at his feet. All of them are desperate for any scrap of his interest. That won't be me. I have no interest in his ways or being compliant to this place.

I'm over the moon to be away from all the prying eyes. I won't lie, I don't want that spotlight on me. It's not a secret that I'm not exactly fond of anyone outside of Aiden, and I suspect the feeling is mutual. I've received many punishments for disagreeing with authority in this place. As well as the hatred of my brothers for my utter lack of respect for Devon.

What a place to call home.

Much to my dislike, this place is my home. I've known

no other. I know it's not normal. It's not like in the books I've read. Once upon a time, I would've had a mother and father, a house to call my own. No doctors and nurses poking and prodding me and dorms full of snoring brothers you can only wish to trust. Well, that's all I can remember.

As we reach our dorm, I sigh in relief. The bulbs of the room are much dimmer than the brightly lit corridors behind us, and the walls are a comforting dark shade of green. My eyes prefer the relief of this darker room, an ache I had barely noticed before beginning to ease away with instant relief.

Twelve beds, all neatly made up with a comforter and a pillow, line the walls with less than a metre between each. I walk past the other beds to my own, collapsing onto my bunk and stretching my arms back to the wall behind me.

We got back without a hitch. I look to my side and give Aiden a toothy grin at our success. Thankful that, for now, it's just the two of us in the room and we might get some peace before tonight.

When there is nothing scheduled, no food, class, or game to be won, we are to amuse ourselves. Without disruption to the doctors above, of course. It is a rarely sanctioned time and I already know exactly what I'm going to do this afternoon as I pull out a book from under my pillow.

Aiden rolls his eyes at me, and I stick my tongue out at him. He goes to speak but wisely decides against it as I glare at him over the pages. I may know the words by heart, but it's such a rare treat to spend time with this book. He knows better than to interrupt.

In my periphery, I notice Aiden clamber onto his bed beside mine. He has one of only two bunks who have the high set windows above them, right at the end of the room. As he goes up onto his tiptoes, I know he's watching the closest form of entertainment we have. People watching.

Green with envy, we could watch as the doctors bring newcomers to the island. Young men and women who are free to roam the outside space where we are not. We observe as they got given individual homes that we are desperate for. Never once having that sense of privacy or home comfort for ourselves.

As time passes on, we realise the differences between us and them. They are disposable and it is, in fact, us who are the lucky ones. We get the longevity. It is all one big test of course. One, I suspect, we failed at when the doctor promised us our own rooms when we were old enough. A bribe. Something we could have done without and probably would have been given anyway. To keep us complacent and following the rules.

I'd prefer more time to hide in my books. That kind of bribery would be far more likely to sway my head. It's a privilege to be allowed to read. We have rules, times, schedules, and uniforms. It would be unthinkable for me to escape inside a book for longer than the allotted time.

There is too much power in knowledge and they can't have that now, can they?

Today I will take this opportunity to read while I can. While Aiden keeps watch on those outside our walls.

AGE ELEVEN

Staying light on my feet, I follow Devon. Long past the medical wing of our home and out the other side to the lab above. He'd spoken of an appointment he had to keep, one I wanted to sneak into. The perfect opportunity to learn what was happening to him and my brothers.

I hadn't expected to be led outside of our facility, and panic clenches my gut at the thought of leaving without permission. Despite the punishment's ineffectiveness on me, something deep inside has me worried that pushing this boundary may be a step too far.

I debate merely seconds as he inputs the code to leave. Watching his hand cover the panel, I realise I can only figure out a couple of the digits. This is my only chance. I decide to follow behind, quickly and quietly, getting through the door before it closes.

I instantly know I made a mistake.

The open corridor holds very few doors for me to hide

behind, and no furnishings. The stark whiteness matching our own walls downstairs makes my black uniform glaringly obvious in the light. As Devon walks onwards, I know I am well and truly stuck until his return.

What is best? To linger here or move onwards. I can hope no one comes to this entrance, then pray Devon feels merciful upon his return to let me back in. I know it's unlikely, but the alternative of following him could be even riskier.

I take the risk; that clawing need to know what is happening drags me onward. Making no sound, I follow Devon at a distance along the rabbit warren of hallways. We come across no others, and for once, luck may be on my side. I might actually get what I want from this task.

Devon stops at a door no different from any of the others. I look around for markings to signpost it as the correct room, but there is nothing. How did he know where to go?

It's too late to move as he turns. His black eyes glint with predatory glee as he flashes me a dark smile over his shoulder. Did he know I was there all along? I don't understand how it's possible, I'm positive there's no way he could have heard me. There's nowhere to go, so I stand by the door, waiting for the inevitable. For the doctor to come and give out whatever punishment I am due.

Minutes pass.

I can't believe Devon hasn't said anything. I press my ear to the door and listen, but I can only hear silence. Cool to the touch, I realise something metal must soundproof the door. I huff a laugh; this entire mission has been a waste of time.

Learning anything this way is impossible. To get any information, I would've needed to be inside the room already. I lean against the opposite wall and slide down its length, sitting with my knees to my chest, completely deflated.

I don't know how long I wait, but when our Doctor finally comes out, his face is one of disappointment. I don't look at him or Devon as I'm route marched back home. A feeling of resentment and anger flares through me. I know he wants me to feel guilty, but it's not me. I have a right to know what it is they are doing to us.

"I am sorry, Rafferty, but obviously the cane is no longer an effective form of punishment on such an inso-lent boy. You're too nosy for your own good. When you are ready, you will understand how important these things are, but until then, you need to reflect on the damage you are doing."

As the Doctor leads me deeper into the maze of corri-dors, I am less confident in where I am. His words sink in, but the chaotic tantrum of lacking control thrums close to the surface. I hate being reminded that I am, in fact, a child. It's been so long since I have been allowed to behave as such and no one can make me feel as small as this man.

The closest things I had to a toy growing up was the baby books we had. Otherwise, it was play-fighting among my brothers and learning to brawl, climb, and run.

Making up games we could play together. Those grew into the dangerous ones we play today.

Could you really consider that a childhood?

Yet, this doctor still insists on calling me a boy, making me feel beneath everyone else. Even Aiden was granted more respect, but he preferred to follow the rules. He will be less than thrilled with my little venture today.

As we enter back to the facility below, my brothers sneer and scoff at me as we pass them. Some come to the dormitory doorways to stare, others already in full view of my shameful walk to punishment. Some follow, eager to witness whatever it is I am going to be subjected to. It's not unusual.

The Doctor stops abruptly, turning to face me. We are in front of a door next to the medical wing, one I've never seen opened before. Looking me up and down, the Doctor sighs, looking almost reluctant. It's strange and makes me a little wary of what's coming.

Pulling a keycard from his trouser pocket, I watch with trepidation as he swipes it against the door. Excited whispers echo the corridor from my brothers as they watch the door swinging forward, a light automatically flicking on.

"In you go, boy. Hopefully, a bit of time alone will give you some insight into what it is you need to do to become more like your brothers."

His words are a jab at the knowledge I'm trying to acquire. The stabbing wound of realisation that every move I make is a test to him. One I am constantly failing each time I strive to find out the information before I am supposed to. It won't stop me from trying. I walk inside, ignoring the laughter that follows behind me.

The door shuts, sealing me inside, shutting me away from the cacophony of sound my brothers make. There's a small window in the door for my brothers to peer through and a large, hinged flap at the bottom. I've become a zoo exhibit for them, but safe and away from the noise of their cackling laughter.

There's only a single bunk and a chamber pot in the otherwise windowless room. I could almost laugh to myself, except a witness might have me removed. He's put me in isolation. It's amusing that he thinks time alone will bother me. It gives me time to process and to plan. He nearly had me worried there.

While I'm locked in this chamber, maybe I can learn to be quiet enough to follow Devon successfully next time. Perhaps I can attempt to retrace my steps in my mind of the confusing layout upstairs, so next time I will be able to make my way back before the appointment starts.

They didn't tell me how long I was to be isolated, but I know I will be fine. It's a shame I don't have access to any paper or books. It would make my musings much easier to follow.

AGE FIFTEEN

It could've been hours, maybe just minutes. Time means nothing once that door slams shut behind you. My white shirt is already damp with sweat and clings to my body. It replaces the black uniform I normally wear. Everything needs to be white in this room.

Thump, thump, thump, the pounding headache starts. It rapidly beats in time with my heart. The organ feels like it wants to rip its way right out of my chest. It's like a thudding rhythm of wild, galloping horses inside my body. I close my eyes and tell myself it's all inside my head. The nothingness behind my lids doesn't quell the fear of what awaits me.

Solitude is becoming an increasing issue.

Each time I'm found, the stakes are raised in my isolation. It started with just those few days. A walk in the park, I'd come out laughing. Then a week, two, a month, and finally six months. It hadn't worked. Removing me from people had been a vacation.

Then they upped the ante.

Instead of time alone in a normal cell, the room I'm currently placed in is devoid of anything but sterile white walls. I've fought back and chased away my gnawing curiosity over time. It didn't matter. Every single time I would crack, the aching need to know caught me in its grip and I'd be back inside this caged hell. I've been here five times before. I know the drill.

Sensory deprivation.

I'm slowly losing all sense of myself.

My head spins, and I lay down on the soft white floor. I stare vacantly at the flap where food will eventually be pushed through. I don't even remember opening my eyes.

Last time they kept me here, it was for six months. It felt like a lifetime. I don't know how long they'll keep me this time. How I'll survive it. Now, I'm starting to wonder if this information is truly worth the price. Is it worth just giving in to their version of reality to escape this?

Can I live with the ruthless violence the doctors want for me?

Now they want me to forget, and I need to keep a grip on any knowledge I have.

Wait, I wanted to give in. Do I?

Laughter pours from me as nonsensical words drift round my mind. I give into the maddening chaos of my head. I curl into myself and hope it can't be worse than this, already knowing it's only just the beginning.

I startle awake as the door slams shut. I watch as a figure looms towards me, shading me briefly from the brightness of the room. It's our Doctor. He's dressed from head to toe in white as he steps closer to me, a medical mask covering his face.

I don't know if he's real or one of the many apparitions my mind conjures. He doesn't speak. I've heard nothing but my own voice for—well, I don't know how long. His blue eyes spark a malice I know too well, and a swell of fear rushes through me.

I watch him wearily, a looming white ghost advancing on me. My heart pounds, and I slowly blink my eyes closed and open again. I want this dream to vanish, to go back into the abyss of my mind, but he keeps moving closer.

The unsuspected prick of the needle brings focus to my arm as crystal clear liquid is pushed into my body. An odd sense of déjà vu takes over my mind momentarily. Before I can question the doctor, he's vanished. It's more likely he was never there at all.

A cool wave of tranquillity hits me. It's so rare, I let myself sink into it.

Sink, sink, sink. Right down into the floor below.

He is deep within me, a prowling presence I know wasn't there before. Unless I truly have cracked. Broken, like they wanted. Snapped into two pieces of the same person. All I know is that my beast inside is waiting to be released from his cage.

We can't stand the white surrounding us any longer.

Hell, even the food is nothing but white rice and water. We want to rip these clothes from our body and lay them to shreds.

My fist slams into the door of this enclosure, refusing to remain imprisoned any longer. I punch again and again until my knuckles bleed. I smear the decadent red across the walls of my chamber, laughing as my beast howls inside with pride.

Before I can raise my bare foot to start my next assault. The door opens. I don't know who opens it, and I don't care. I smell the fresh air on the breeze and see sunlight filter through the end of the corridor.

With freedom in my sight, I run.

CHAPTER 7

SOLOMON

Age Sixteen

I thought I'd gotten out of the shit, but it turns out the only way I can run is into more trouble. Taking the overnight train had meant to be my salvation, my way out from a lifetime of hurt and abandonment. Away from a dad who doesn't give a damn and a mum who is checked out. I know it isn't their fault, not really.

PTSD is hell, especially for those without any help.

Both my parents served in the military before I was born. They met on assignment abroad; I don't know where exactly. They don't talk to me about it, about anything really. I'm pretty convinced whatever happened when they were serving was bad though. Horrendous enough that it had damaged them beyond repair. Enough that they weren't suited for parenthood. It wasn't like I was planned anyway.

A mistake.

When I was younger, there had been times when things had been good. Where we could be a normal, happy family. As I got older, those times became fewer and further between. I can't remember the last time I'd seen them happy. In my parents' more manic episodes, they forgot they even had a kid.

I don't think they'll even notice I'm gone.

My mum would be too strung out on whichever medication or recreational drug she can get her hands on. My dad would stare angrily at the walls as if they were the reason for all his troubles with a beer in hand. Each zoned out of reality in their own ways. Forever leaving me behind.

Even when I was young, they left me for days, learning to fend for myself between each episode. Stuck inside our two-bedroom apartment, rummaging through the food I could prepare to eat. Keeping as quiet as possible to not disturb my parents in one of their moods.

When I was tall enough to unlock the highest bolt across the front door to our dingy flat, I was free to venture out by myself. By then, my abrasive attitude and odd characteristics had already formed. By missing so much school, I didn't learn how to socialise with the other kids. Didn't know what the social norms were. I was the weird one, the angry one, the bad one. I couldn't help but pick up these problematic behaviours from my parents.

Since I can remember, both are prone to waking up in the night screaming. The nightmares are so intense they fight out, kicking and punching anyone who dares to go near them. I learned the hard way it was better to leave them to sleep than to try and wake them.

As much as I hate my parents, I love them too. I don't blame them for the things they did or didn't do. Deep down, I know it's not their fault. Even so, for years now, all my thoughts have focused on leaving the toxic environment I lived in.

Self-reliant in ways most teenagers my age wouldn't understand; I knew I had to leave. Any money I earned got saved up, preparing me for my new life. I know I am independent and resourceful. I have grown up too fast, but I am going to be free from that place. Last night, I thought I was finally going to leave. I had my ticket; I was on the train. I was gone.

I don't remember closing my eyes.

Lying here awake, I know everything has changed. There's no way I got here from the train alone. Jagged stones beneath my body are a harsh reality check into this new nightmare I've landed in. The sunshine beats down from a cloudless sky across my unknown surroundings, while waves breach the rocks slowly sweeping towards me.

I know I'll need to move soon, but shock has overtaken my body. My mind is not complying with logic. I should still be on the train; I had been so close to my freedom. My independence, not whatever this is.

I feel around me, searching for the backpack I had taken with me on my journey the night before, and come across nothing. Sighing, I push myself upright, my muscles and joints creaking in protest, making me wonder just how long I have been in this position. My shoulders sag as I look around and see it's empty of my precious things. Someone has taken it.

It's not the clothes I'm bothered by, or hell, even the bit of money I'd ruthlessly saved up so I could leave. It was the little mementos, the photos of those times when my parents were actually a family to me, now long gone, lost to me, that has a lump forming in my throat. There are no second copies of those pictures. No proof those times ever existed outside of my memory.

Giving myself a moment, I shut my eyes, taking in a deep shuddery breath. I just need to remember I'm alive. That is the most important thing in this situation. I concentrate on my breathing for a few brief minutes, letting go of not only the grief of losing my planned escape but also my family pictures.

Now is not the time to lose my temper.

First thing I need to do is find the fucker who did this. Only then can I lose my shit. Getting to my feet, I look in both directions along the beach and ponder which route I should take. I discount the dense forest behind me, it will be easier to spot others out in the open on the beach. In this weather, there's bound to be someone walking a dog or something, right?

At random, I choose to go right, following along next to the lapping waves of the shore. I try to ignore the biting pinch of the stones cutting into my bare feet that brings attention to the obvious. Whoever brought me here took my shoes too. I wade into the water, the cool ocean soothing my feet. The sharp pebbles crushed down into smoother shards and eventually into sand as I let the water raise to my knees.

I don't know how long I've been following the shore, but I'm yet to see any sign of others. It's starting to look like this is an undiscovered deserted island, which is completely nuts. I mean, someone must have brought me here, so there must be others, right?

I can't be alone.

Maybe I took the wrong direction? Maybe I should have gone left. I might have ended up at some island resort and found myself in luxury. I scoff to myself, knowing the possibility of that is still unlikely. However much I wish for it.

Noises from the treeline have me spinning to face them, peering into the dense thicket of trees. Is it an animal, or people that has me so tense? I don't know which I hope for most. I've been walking for a few hours now at least, and the intensity of the sun hasn't let up. My mind is a little less than on top form.

Fatigue is immense, with my muscles burning from continuous use. My skin cracks and peels from the heat, but I've not relented, I have to continue on until I find someone. The cover of the shade sounds nice, but in the time I've been splashing the water's edge, my mind wanders to how I came to be here. The ideas ruminating inside my head have been nothing outside of horrific to what lies further inland.

"Hello?"

I instantly feel stupid for calling out. Why couldn't I just keep quiet and keep a vigilant watch? I'm like that one character in those horror movies. The one who has the murderer jump out at them the next minute and I can't believe I just did that; I'm so going to die.

"Hey, who is that?" A male voice shouts back from the trees. They don't sound too old. Maybe it's another teenager like me, but why are they lurking in the shade of the forest rather than out in the sun? Something seems incredibly wrong with this situation.

"Come out here, show yourself," I yell back, not liking the fact they remain hidden. My stomach is in knots with nervous energy. I wade to the water's edge, aware of the danger lurking, and how the waves will not aid me should I need to run.

"Okay, but my friends would rather stay in the shadows, much cooler for them. It's too hot out in the sun," his tone is smug, making me tense. A bare-chested boy around my age steps out from the trees, thick hair falling into his eyes. As he moves into the sun, I catch sight of multiple lines scoring one of his arms. Deep red slashes gorged out of his flesh, looking like a blade intentionally sliced through them. I shudder.

As he steps out, multiple fires light inside the trees, lighting up the shadows of many figures. I take a splashing step away as the boy walks closer towards me, his eyes lighting up with amusement and malice. I try to count the figures, but as the lights bob and sway, I realise they must be holding torches. It appears like they are numerous, especially when the cackles and yells follow my movement as I back away further.

"Stay back," I stammer. I frantically look around me, wondering what I should do. Everything in my gut is screaming at me not to trust this gang with there being so many. I move to the shore; glad I'd had the foresight to move closer earlier and start to edge even further from the boy before me.

His eyes track my every movement.

"Hey, over here! This way!" My head spins to the voice and I catch sight of two figures in the distance waving towards me frantically. I have two choices: the wiry teenager with his flaming entourage ahead of me or these two calling for me along the beach. Both could be traps, or neither, but I follow my instincts and race up the pebbled beach.

Howls and jeers follow my pounding footsteps, the rocks once again slicing into my bare feet. Their crashing footfalls behind me keeps my pace fast, desperate to escape them. A large stone crashes into the water, splashing by my feet, then another splaying stone just behind me. I swerve as they launch projectiles in a continuous barrage. Large rocks and fiery wood barely missing me as I dodge back and forth.

As I come closer to the two figures, I notice the men behind are further away. Maybe lacking the stamina to keep up with my speed and desperation to escape, although the main boy is still on my trail.

Ahead of me, the two boys gesture for me to follow them into the trees, and I do so without thought. I have no choice now, trap or not. I fling myself after them, keeping them in my eyesight and hope to lose my entourage behind.

I don't know how long we run, how far, but as I start to stumble and trip, my body heavy with exhaustion, I know I can't keep moving for much longer. I strain my ears and as far as I can tell, we've lost the men from behind.

"Hey. They've given up," I yell out, as I slow to a stop. I bend down, putting my hands on my knees and let out heaving breaths. The crunch of leaves underfoot alerts me to the approach of the others, and I stand upright once more. I watch as the two boys step closer towards me, one tucked just behind the other.

"Thanks, I appreciate your help there. I'm Solomon," I smile, sticking my hand out to the blonde boy. He eyes me for what seems like a lifetime before eventually taking my palm into his own. His grip is firm, and I find myself questioning who this guy really is.

Peeking from around behind this wall of muscle is a

kid. Kind of scrawny looking, clinging onto the guy's other hand so tight his knuckles go white with the strain. It doesn't take a genius to realise he is scared.

I take a step back from the two, giving the kid some space to breathe. His shoulders relax, though only slightly, as his deep green eyes study me. His emerald depths almost piercing my soul as I shift from foot to foot, unused to such scrutiny.

"I'm Huck and this is Dario. Glad we ran into you when we did. I'm not sure you would've made it otherwise," Huck says, his face sombre. Hazel eyes cast a look over Dario, who gives a firm nod. "Come on, let's get you home. It's safer there. There is a lot you'll need to learn."

He's not wrong. Though safe isn't exactly a word I'd use. I rather think of it as a prison.

CHAPTER 8

RAFFERTY

Age Eighteen

It's taken a while to readjust to life since I left the confines of solitary. A year inside the same four walls successfully did its damage and I still bear the scars. I wouldn't survive it again. I'm lucky to have remained sane. Though am I truly sane? That split is still inside of me. One that widens more and more each day.

A purring contentment growls in the back of my mind as I stroll through the forest. No longer confined to the walls of the facility. The Doctor says I've become mature enough to leave, to run free. I don't trust his motivations, but the temptation of it is too great to question.

My beast is a constant reminder of where I've been and of the differences between me and my brothers. The growling, howling monster lurking within my mind, giving its opinions when I don't ask for them. Always needing that satisfaction of freedom and companionship.

I've told no one about him. Not even Aiden.

The risk seems too high. It's not that I don't trust Aiden. The walls here have ears, and I can't risk being made into an experiment. It's not exactly below this place. Hell, maybe the other half of myself is some experimentation gone wrong. I won't be parted with him now.

The doctors have taken my other brothers off the island today, and it's only us who stalk the woodland. Animals don't seem to sense us; they remain still until our soundless stalking footsteps approach too closely. My body is primed to chase, to hunt, to play, but I suppress the urge, despite his rumbling protest of displeasure.

I am not an animal. Not like my brothers.

Since I have been gone, their fight has become one of dominance. One that Devon has easily taken control of. There's a darkness inside my brother, one I fear has become rotten to the core. I had once thought he may become a problem, now I know he is one.

His dominance controls the others, seeing how they all fit into the pack. This time next week I'll get my chance to prove myself. I'll be going with my brothers to see exactly what it is they do when they leave the island. What gets them so hyped up, and let my beast have his fill. For the only thing I have been told is that when they leave, they hunt.

AGE EIGHTEEN - A FEW MONTHS LATER

I don't let the deafening shriek of the siren penetrate my mind as I lock down my prey. Readying myself for the hunt. I don't let the growls, hisses, and grunts inside my mind affect my decision. If I wanted his opinion, I'd ask. He needs this as much as I do. It's been months since the first hunt, and nothing would steer me off course.

The blaring noise is a signal for them to run and hide. Their only warning to escape us. To those that even bother to try anymore. My Wildcat has never given up her fight. I wait long minutes for the silence to overtake the screeching din, my target never wavering.

I tilt my head and watch as my auburn-haired prey steadily runs for the treeline. Slowly, this girl has sunk into my skin. She's an obsession. A passion I can't let go of. I'm fixated on her as she attaches herself to every molecule of my being. Fate brought me to her, to protect her until she is ready. I will never let another lay a hand upon what is mine.

I stalk, I hunt, I catch, but I could never let myself harm her. She's far too precious to allow anyone to damage her pale skin. She's a beauty in the making, a delicate soul that is no more than thirteen. Her skin is sallow, and her body is nothing more than a toothpick. I desperately want the chance to help her, to wrap her in my arms, but this is all I can do.

For now.

My eyes skim to the left, catching Devon's gaze that also follows her. Violence brims through my veins. My beast howls, begging to be released. Despite the games we played as children and the tendencies of my brothers, they do not encourage us to inflict violence on one another any longer. Someone has thinned enough of our herd.

If he hurts my Wildcat, I won't be held accountable.

I snarl in his direction. Devon's cruel face turns to me, taunting darkness in his eyes. He'd been to this island long before I had. Muliercula, an island entirely filled with kidnapped girls and women. Back when I'd been suffering in the white room, he'd been here hunting the women of Muliercula; it's a whole new level to the games we'd once played.

When I saw her, strong, confident and wild, I knew she was something special. I have been told she hadn't always been so. Muliercula changed her irreparably. With just one look, she caught me. My soul had cried out that she was mine, and my beast had wholeheartedly agreed. We needed her like the oxygen we breathed, and we would have her.

One day.

When I had finally been allowed in on the secrets my brothers already knew, the damage to my Wildcat had already been done. Devon had been the first, and the others followed in his wake. Devon saw my fixation right away, and she became a shiny new toy once again in his eyes. He had a new quest: to destroy her personally.

So far, he'd failed.

He mocks me at every turn. Repeating the vile things he had done to her, the things my other brothers did as she wept. I held my tongue as I listened to him spew his hatred. Walking away as his cruel laughter followed. She had been lucky to survive.

I'd caught the remnants of his victims before. Some had been left for dead, broken, bruised and bloodied. Unable to walk again where he'd destroyed them. It was a kindness to kill his victims, rather than leave them to suffer. Her, along with others, he'd just taken what he'd needed to sate his ruthless desires and left them in his wake.

After all, it wasn't easy to kidnap new victims every day to replace his toys.

The siren cuts out, and it's my cue to move. To prepare, I sniff the air, catching hold of her vanilla scent before pushing myself forward. I know her tricks. I've learned them over the months, but it's more fun to take the time to hunt her. To track her moves and follow her paths. I know she never runs in a straight line; she will double back on herself and make false tracks.

She might be young, but my Wildcat has power in her knowledge. So far that has kept her far from Devon's grasp. In her time here, she's learned as much about us as I have about her. It's so exhilarating to learn each and every new thing.

I know this isn't normal. I know my obsession with hunting is wrong. Hell, it's how I was raised, but chasing her? I'll never stop. I would follow her to the ends of the earth. The time isn't right. She's too young right now, but things could change.

They will change.

Five years is fast for someone who has spent forever in a sea of white walls. Where time means nothing at all. It's funny if I followed the rules like my brothers, I probably would have ended up in the same place I am now. With no mental wounds from the white room but with their taste for blood, and desire for these women's bodies. Though Aiden doesn't seem to either.

So who knows?

What I know is, the path I took will lead me somewhere different from them all. It's a journey I have to keep on following, even if I don't like everything that's on it. I need to keep going and hope it leads to freedom. I just hope there's not something crucial I let myself forget in the depths of white.

I can't go back.

Not again.

The place of white walls and madness caused a schism in my mind. One that created this stalking beast in the back of my head. The one who is urging me onwards, pushing us towards our Wildcat.

My booted feet hit the pebbled shore of a beach far from the camp where the women live. I'd missed the sun sinking in the sky, the moon rising behind clouded skies, so engrossed in following her trail. In the wind, I know Devon isn't far behind me. I'd heard screams of a woman not long back and I wonder if he's become bored with his mission this time. His patience is lacking. Unlike my own.

I walk along the water's edge as her scent lingers and disappears. Clever girl. I smile, looking behind me towards the darkened trees. It's as if she knows our senses are much more powerful than her own. Not for the first time, she's used water to hide her smell.

My eyes adjust. Letting the darkness sweep into my sights. Time to start the hunt once more.

Four days it has taken me to find her.

It's the longest it has ever taken; for any of us to find one of our prey. She is an intelligent one, so small, yet utterly perfect.

Now, looking down at my little Wildcat, curled up in sleep, so precious, I can't help but want to reach out and touch her. I silently crouch above her form, watching as she breathes steadily. Chest rising and falling, slow and even. My fingers itch to touch her face, her pale skin almost translucent in the dark night. Full lips, petite nose and dark lashes kissing her skin.

I'm mesmerised.

Mine. My beast hums out his approval. *Ours.* She might not know it yet, but this little thing has captured us as much as we have captured her. One day, things are going to change around here.

Her blue eyes startle open as I push the needle into her neck.

"Caught you, Wildcat."

CHAPTER 9

NIXI

Age Seventeen

"God, kid, I swear you're only here to cause me trouble," Chris grumbles under her breath as she rolls her striking green eyes at me. The tone holds a hint of affection I know so well, despite her complaints. I smile up at her as we walk down the path leading towards the beach where I'd first been abandoned.

It's been a complicated few years.

When I'd first met Chris, I can admit the older girl scared me shitless with her sly smirk and aggressive posture. Now, I know she's all bark and no bite. She still has her quirks, but who doesn't? Chris has helped me out on my mission to help the newest girls acquaint themselves with their new lives here on the island.

"You know you wouldn't have it any other way. Keep up. It has to be any day now, and I want to get there before Aggs has a chance to let the poor girl die. *Again*," I say with a frown. I pick up my pace, knowing that if she gets to her first, it's likely she'll hide the girl from me. It's happened a few times now.

Aggs is a complex creature, and I'd been told she had only gotten worse since Fliss was taken. Like I'd suspected, she had been leaving the new girls out on the beach to die. Alone, starving, and dehydrated. Not even giving the poor things a humane death, they had suffered. Their bodies were washed out to sea or picked apart by the scavenging creatures of this island.

I'd only found out through chance alone. Following my suspicion, I had followed Aggs into the wilderness and across the island on one of her scouting missions. Peering through bushes, I had watched in horror as the woman tossed a young blood covered body into the sea without an ounce of emotion.

"You think she knows we're here?" Chris quickens her stride, her longer legs matching my pace as we hasten to reach the beach.

"Almost certainly, but she won't like coming out in this weather. At least we have that advantage," Chris huffs a response, not liking the weather any better than she likes Aggs. I look to the sky at the greying clouds above, heavy with unfallen rain. My limbs are icy and littered with goosebumps, and I wish, for the hundredth time, I had a jumper or jacket to help shield me from the cold. Wind blows through my hair and pulls at the hem of my white dress. It spreads the chill deeper into my bones. I wrap my arms around my waist as I try to shield myself.

"Come on! Before we get soaked. Better than the sunburn at least," I grumble. Chris bursts out laughing, mirth shining in her emerald eyes.

"Oh god, you looked like a lobster. It was hilarious," Chris cackles back and I can't help but join in with her laughter; infectious and rare.

"Gee, thanks," I grin back sarcastically as I pick up my pace to a jog for the beach. I can just see it coming through the trees in the distance. In minutes, we make it to the edge of the beach, raindrops beginning to pelt down on us unevenly in large drops.

We get to the sandy shore just in time to watch as a boat sails away. An unconscious girl left on the beach in its wake. Left open to the elements without a care. It's not the first time I've caught sight of the white sailboat cruising past the island. I had thought it just delivered new shipments to the warehouse, its crew normally out of sight below.

Not this time.

Standing on the deck is someone I considered far more beast than man. A demon in human guise. His lips tilt in his cruel smile, black hair whipping in the wind as his black eyes—those endless pits of hell—stare out at us.

I shudder.

Wet sand sticks to the soles of my feet, and with Chris hot on my heels, I race over to the girl. Turning my back to the sea, I direct my attention to the teenager. Older than most. Maybe around sixteen. The girl is a pretty thing with brunette curls and a small waist; she'll be eaten alive. Ignoring the rain splashing heavier down upon us, I watch as her chest rises and falls steadily. Her forehead is cool to the touch, but she seems okay. Just out of it from the drugs they've given her. I smile at our luck at getting to her on time.

"I got her," Chris says. As she picks the girl up in bridal style, I can't help rolling my eyes at her. I swear the woman is forever proving herself stronger than anyone else here. It's true the woman is a force to be reckoned with, but I'm always happy to help her. I hide the small smirk as she sinks slightly in the sand with the added weight.

"Come on, let's get her back to camp. It's freezing."

Alice.

Such a pretty name. She woke up about half an hour ago. She gave us insignificant details of the things she remembered: where she'd come from, who she was. I was nearly right about her age; she's actually fifteen. Going by the things she's told us about the outside world, I've worked out I must be about seventeen.

That means I've been here for five years. The realisation is disturbing. I've had to bear five years of this cruel life already, and any chance of escaping is impossible. My hope crushed, and long forgotten.

Now as we sit by my small fire, I consider what it is I have to say to her. I can almost repeat the speech on autopilot now, robotic and clinical, but necessary. A story, not one for children at bedtime, but my story. A warning of what is to come. I try not to sugarcoat it, but equally, I also can't go into the details of every moment of that night.

It hurts too much.

"The first time I heard the siren sound, everyone scattered without explanation. I'd been innocent in every sense of the word. The only woman who'd taken me under her wing that week had scurried off without a whispered warning or a backwards glance. She slammed the door not only in my face but also on our tentative friendship. I had already felt the ugly wounds the women of this camp could carve. Yet, that cut had sliced me the deepest. Abandoned at a campfire in the centre of this little village, the rest already disappeared to the trees while I waited, left deserted for the unknown."

Alice sits opposite me, listening attentively and taking in every word I say. It doesn't matter to her that my voice comes out mechanically. She understands. I can see the pain etched in her face as tears silently run down her face.

Sensing the waves of underlying tension coming from her, I know that she understands where this is going. Knows what is coming for her. It's in the stillness of her body as her breathing almost stops.

"My fate was sealed. I'd only been twelve when I was raped for the first time." My voice is strained as I speak. A pained cry rips from Alice's throat, her hands coming to her mouth, her shoulders shaking violently as she's overcome by anguished sobs. I give her a few minutes to understand the situation of why I'm telling her this story. To fully comprehend what is going to happen to her.

In a way, Alice's age makes things easier. It might make me a monster, but the last girl had only been eight. I had been the one to explain things to such a young child. I could almost understand the other women's reluctance to try, but what was worse: knowing or not knowing?

I close my eyes, shutting out the world surrounding me for just a moment. Soft hands gently take my own, squeezing them in thanks. I take a deep breath, opening my lids once more, looking back into hers to continue gifting my knowledge.

"This place is a different world. Not only do our bodies get defiled but violated by poisons too. Each time the siren rings out, we are given an injection. I'd been at camp not even a week, but not one person bothered to tell me what was going on, what was going to happen or what to expect. I found out the hard way that everyone here was in it for themselves. We're friends, but only to an extent. Once that shrill tone rang out, that was it, you were on your own. I want that to change."

"It needs to change; I can't believe you went through that alone. I'm so sorry," she replies softly. It's not her pity, or her understanding I want. Despite her offering it so freely, a fact I know will be needed in the coming days. I raise my hand to stop her, so I can continue the last threads of my speech.

"Now I need you to understand, I'm trying to change things little by little. I can't change what happens to us, none of us can do much about that." I give her a sad smile. "What I do is to get the girls as they arrive, like I did for you today. So I can prepare you for what's coming. Give you that extra little support I never had. In return, when new girls come, I want you to do the same for them. I need you all to lean on one another, help each other. Do you understand?"

"I do, and I want to help any way I can."

"Another of your lost little pups has arrived, I see," Aggs sneers down at me, her eyes squinting as she looms above me. She wants me intimidated, and it frustrates her that I'm not. Steam practically billowing from her ears.

Ignoring her presence, I glance over to the left,

checking on the others. The small group we've saved from death is currently over with Chris at a fire. They're safe. They haven't noticed the commotion going on over here. I'd like to keep it that way.

Sitting alone next to my run-down shack on the stone step I built myself, I finally acknowledge Aggs' presence. Resting both arms above her on an overhanging branch above my shack, Aggs eyes me nastily. I raise an eyebrow, checking the branches' sturdiness. This tree has done me well so far, keeping my home safe from natural causes.

Shame it couldn't keep people away.

My eyes narrow, trying to figure out her game. I wouldn't put it past her to knock my shack down. It's not the first time she's pulled this kind of stunt. Aggs stretches, leaning down towards me, applying more weight to the wood, the bark creaking in protest. Maybe she's trying to pull the branch down onto my home this time.

I look around, noting none of her friends are surrounding us to cheer her on with taunting jabs. In fact, it's just me and her in this quiet area of the village. It's a new move for her to come at me with no mocking hyenas at her heels.

I'm almost impressed.

I know there are words her little minions would never believe. No, the words that she liked to spew could never come from the almighty Aggs' mouth. I'd tried to tell them before. Of course, they had never believed me. Her venom has only gotten worse over the years.

"What do you want, Aggs?"

"Just being friendly is all. Another newbie. Pretty one, isn't she? That devil is going to eat her right up. He left the little one crying for days. I'm sure he's desperate for something with a little more fight. Bit more like you, so I heard."

Her laughter is a nasty dark thing that claws at my skin. Bile creeps up my throat as I glare daggers her way. The devil, as she calls him. The one with black eyes and blacker hair, whose desire is others utmost agony and despair. He matches Aggs more than any other, and even then, I wouldn't wish his merciless soul on anyone.

Not even her.

Aggs would happily push someone down to get herself away when the sirens ring out. It was her decision to let all newcomers remain unaware. It was her decision to allow the girls to become cannon fodder. Never actually stopping anyone from being caught in the end, but at least the ones who run get a head start. I will never understand the logic of her madness.

I'm certain hers had been amongst the screams that first night and many, many times since. If it weren't for that, I'd swear she was part of the sadistic mess of people who keep us here. She certainly has the tendencies. I let out a shudder, trying to forget the images that revolve round my mind. Time after time, I painstakingly fought battles, that in the end, had not been worth fighting.

"I don't think I will ever understand you, Aggs," I comment. Doing nothing but stare at the woman, trying to piece together what makes this woman tick. My eyes flit across her broad frame and up to her eyes. They burn back at me with such hatred that I almost recoil. Once, she had been able to make me shudder with fear. Now I stand strong. She is bigger than me and that is her advantage, but she no longer scares me. There are things much more frightening out there than this woman.

She is just a bully.

Aggs makes her move, taking a menacing step closer to me. She wraps a fist around my messy auburn hair. The tangles knot between her fingers. I slam my hand onto hers, trying in vain to remove her grip, but it's useless. This bully wants to take me down, but I won't go down without fighting back.

Like a kitten raised indignantly by its scruff, she raises me by my hair. Strands rip violently from my scalp. My eyes blur with tears. My nails bite into her skin, but she refuses to let go. Up on my toes that barely scrape the ground, I slip on the slick mud beneath me. Letting out another anguished cry as a chunk of hair is ripped out into her grasp.

"I always knew I should've left you on that beach to rot. Word to the wise little girl. Stop trying to cross me." Spittle hits my face as she hisses her words. Wrenching her grip from my hair, she slings me, sending my back crashing into my makeshift shelter. She storms off, leaving me to deal with the fallout of her destruction. I don't need to look; I felt it. Knowing already that my home is once again a crumpled pile of metal, wood and plastic.

What a fucking waste.

Sitting up, I pull my legs to my chest, rest my forehead on my knees, and sigh deeply. A headache can be added to my list of joys for today. Just another day in paradise. I lift my head at the faint sound of padding feet to see Alice approaching.

"She did a number on you, huh?" I nod. As she sits opposite me, her cheeks turn a bright shade of red and my face morphs into a look of confusion. What has her so flustered?

"Oh I, I didn't mean to look but...," she squeaks. Rattled, Alice waves a hand at my legs. I can't help but to grin. Hell, my legs had mostly got me covered, and she's all upset about my dress riding up showing a bit of skin. I hadn't even noticed. Definitely going to need to take her to the bathing pool when it's quieter, or we could have a problem. Can't have her not washing.

"Sorry, you forget about modesty around here," I shrug, but lower my legs, covering myself back up so she's more comfortable. She'd get used to it soon enough. Poor kid. The girl was lucky that me and Chris had changed from our wet clothes after the storm earlier or she'd have had even more of an eyeful. White dresses with no bras or knickers. It was a no-brainer which species had made that decision when supplies were organised.

Any smile I had vanishes at the realisation that this is all so new to her, and after the story I gave her today, it's going to be a really rough adjustment period. It's been so long since I'd been that frightened, broken little girl and I really tried to forget it was me in the story I told. It's part of why I had to get it out without interruption. There's no time to think it through.

"Hey, you okay?" Alice's voice breaks through my thoughts.

"Aren't I supposed to be asking you that?" I deflect the question back at her and she chuckles. The kid seems sweet; I hope it's something she doesn't lose.

I let out a startled squeak at the roar of the siren suddenly shrieking through the air. My heart stutters and I look up at a wide-eyed Alice. The fear in her hazel eyes looks as deeply embedded as my own, but we can't stop this, despite the lack of time to prepare. It's here.

"Shit, there's no more time. I'm sorry. Quickly, come with me." I jump to my feet, cursing the bastards. They never blare the siren this early after they have brought a new girl to the island. I grip her hand, tug her to her feet, and drag her behind me. We pass swiftly across the camp with our hands clenched tightly together as women run inside their homes. Others run out into the woods. Panic is etched onto their faces and the beat of chaotic footfalls and shrieking tones fill the air in a riotous cacophony.

"Was it like this your first time?" Alice's nervous voice penetrates the noise.

"It's always this way. The silence is worse. Keep moving," I demand, not meaning to scare her, but the time is now. I only have one last thing I can offer her, and it'll be her choice of what she does after that.

I lead her to a patch of mint leaves. A specific herb I planted long ago at the edge of camp. A trick I'd learned, through whispers of the women. One's who gave up long ago having been here the longest. Surrounding the purple and white flowers in front of us are large mint leaves to be eaten. It helps blunt the mind if the right quantity is ingested.

Of course, I'd tested the theory, making sure they weren't just bullshitting me before digging the plant up and replanting it near to camp. Thankfully, it had flourished. I now make certain it's something I advise all the newcomers to use, even when the flower isn't in bloom. Picking several of the leaves, I pass them to her.

"Chew them thoroughly or it won't work. It will help numb your mind to what's going on. I'm so sorry. I need to go, but can I do anything before then?" She pulls me towards her, hugging me briefly in a tight embrace, before pushing me away. Sob catching in her throat, tears already falling, she's not ready, but she has to be.

"I'll be okay, go." Her words are a lie, but one I have to let myself believe. As I turn and run to the dense woods, I hear her echoing thanks twisting around the air, entangling into the siren's call. I try not to let the guilt linger when I don't turn back. At least I gave her all the preparations I could before the inevitable.

She would survive this.

CHAPTER 10

SOLOMON

Age Seventeen

I am done.

Gathering my things together, I fume at once again having Huck treating me as a glorified bodyguard to his precious Dario. I am sick and fucking tired of it, and I won't take it anymore. I rip my bag open, throwing a couple of cans into my pack. They crash loudly together, and I curse, hoping the ring-pulls remain intact as I stuff more of my belongings inside.

"He didn't mean it."

I startle, looking up at Dario across the fire, his voice

echoing around the cave. Only a year younger than me, his frame is so much smaller. Slender and short, you could mistake him for a child rather than the teenager he is. In fact, when I'd first met him, clutching Huck's hand so tightly, I had thought just that. A kid. Well, except for his eyes, I could tell those green orbs had already seen so much.

I huff a non-response back, returning to my packing. Too angry to reply to anything either of my companions has to say. I was a waste of resources if I didn't help Huck. He had made that perfectly clear. I have always been happy to help with any task put forward to me. Problem is, that the only thing he ever asks me to do is guard Dar. Not that I mind his company, but it's not a life I wanted.

So when Huck said I was useless, he had meant it. Purely because I had asked to do something else with my time. If I even suggest a plan on how to get off this island, he gets himself into a little hissy fit. Telling me how dangerous it would be, how futile. Well, I'm sorry if I want to try—not to cower in fear.

I cannot deal a moment longer in this cutesy little love nest with Dario and Huck. The two of them are completely infatuated with one another, but also in complete denial. Hell, maybe they really don't realise it. If they don't, they are the only ones, and I am sick and tired of being their buffer. Their safety blanket stopping them from crossing some unknown boundary.

"You're really going then?" Huck snipes at me as he walks in, his eyes flaring with undisguised fury.

"Nothing for me here, is there? It's not like you give a shit about me, is it?" I look over to Dario, my dig obviously hitting its mark as he flinches. Sorrow covers his face, and I try to ignore the guilt gnawing at me. It's not his fault.

It's hard. Part of me knows I'm being unreasonable. It's not such a big deal keeping an eye out for the smaller boy. The problem is, I'm used to doing things for myself. I've done it for so long that it's become second nature to me. Now, doing this, helping others. Being involved in that group dynamic is so foreign to me it's become unbearable. Never getting to have that time on my own, to refocus my mind and thoughts.

It's intolerable.

"You're so selfish," Huck barks at me as I storm past him, smashing my shoulder into his as I pass. I just want him to shut up. To leave me alone for just one damn minute, but he never does. Always baiting me, flicking the flint to spark that flame of anger inside me. I ignore their harsh whispered voices echoing behind me as I hurry down the unlit tunnel.

"Sol, wait a minute," Dario's voice calls out as I step outside into the early morning sunlight. His footfalls slapping on the ground beneath him. I blink away the spots dancing in my vision as I decide on what to do. I sigh, knowing that I can't deny him the chance to at least speak before I leave.

"What do you want?" I try to keep the growling anger from my tone as he catches up to me.

"Let me help you find another cave. You don't need to go outside of the group completely. Just find your own space," he says, his face almost pleading. His eyes were wide, innocent, and filled with hope. Damn, he's perfected the puppy dog eyes.

Looking across the rocky landscape of our home, I can't see a single reason to say no. From the past year on this insane island, I know there's no other safe haven. Well, unless I want to become one of them. Those savages are hardly human.

I've gotten myself into a couple of scrapes with the men on the other side of the island since I first arrived. The ones who cut lines into their flesh. I can't help the crawling shudder that takes over my body. I've been lucky, but to survive out on my own would be difficult.

That's not even considering the ones that inject us. I've yet to find their hiding spot.

"Don't think he's coming in with me. I'm not dealing with this one's trouble like you do." I glower at Peter as he steps closer from his own cave entrance where he's clearly been lurking. The blonde boy eavesdropping on things that don't concern him, as per usual. This guy has been a thorn in my side ever since I arrived, always putting me down, being a little sneak and telling tales.

"He said my own cave. Not share one, so don't worry your pretty little head." I smile at him sardonically, hoping to get him off my case.

"Just making sure you understand. It's not like your intelligence is likely to win any awards. Well, unless it's for stupidity and getting into situations requiring rescue. How many times has Huck needed to get you out of shit?"

I ignore Peter's taunting question. So what if a couple of times was under-exaggerating? No one got hurt while I tried to find ways off this island. I just got caught up with the crazies once in a while. It's not like I asked Huck to help me either. He just always seemed to know.

"Ha, you don't even have the decency to answer now. You know I'm right," his mocking laughter would once have made me angry, but I find myself strangely calm.

"Shut up, Peter," Huck speaks from behind me, a hand landing on my shoulder. I should have known despite our fight; despite our differences, he would always have my back.

"He's doing what he feels he must. What did you do when you first got here, piss yourself? At least he's doing something meaningful," Huck says. I look around, my face turning to meet his, and he nods. I return the gesture. "Come on, let's find you somewhere that we won't drive each other mad."

Although he doesn't apologise for his harsh words earlier, he doesn't need to. His actions speak louder than words ever could. The three of us walk away from a gaping Peter who stomps his way back inside his cave like a petulant child.

Dario, as always, takes hold of Huck's hand without thought, and I can't help but smile. I hope one day they work out just how much they actually mean to one another.

AGE EIGHTEEN

I sit cross-legged outside my cave, looking across at my two friends with a small smile on my face. They still haven't figured it out yet, either that or they're purposefully ignoring what is obvious to every other person.

Huck and Dario want each other *badly*.

I am so happy to no longer be their constant cock-block. The sexual tension in that cave had been so intense it was in danger of destroying our friendship completely. They still drive me to the brink of insanity, but I now find different ways of cooling my temper down before blowing up at them.

Mostly, at least.

Watching as Huck leans over Dario possessively, crowding him into the stone wall, shouldn't be as insanely hot as it is. I can't help but imagine that Huck is a dirty bastard, growling all these nasty things to innocent little Dario as he blushes so prettily.

Dar is the epitome of pure, his face reddening at any implication of something even remotely sexual, and I've seen Huck's reaction to him. His face turns into something almost sinful as he readjusts himself. His movements become progressively more possessive and powerful, and like now, he'll quickly find a way to be close to his green-eyed obsession.

They are my friends, but what can I say, except I'm eighteen, stuck alone on an island with all males? It's not like I haven't heard what some of the other guys get up to in these caves. I ignore my throbbing cock as I watch my friends, hoping for once they finally get the nerve to take this thing they have to the next level.

Not for my sake, but for their own.

"For fuck's sake," I hiss out in a whisper, smacking my thighs as I watch a nervous Dario slink his way under Hucks' arm. A coy smile on his face as he talks like nothing is different between them. He grabs Huck's hand like he always does, and they walk into their cave.

"They'll get there eventually." I jump, his voice not one I was expecting. It feels like most of the people here can barely tolerate me. I'm normally left to my own devices. I guess it's why I get into so much trouble.

"What the hell do you want, Rafferty?"

"You know the deal. Sirens ring in an hour and I thought I'd stop by for a visit before then." Raff's reply shocks me. I stand, maybe I'll get going. I'm not used to the extra head start. He looks me up and down, his eyes briefly pausing at my hard cock before looking up at my eyes. The heat rushes to my face, but I can't read his expression as his eyes glint back at me.

"Sit, talk with me for a while. You know nothing can happen to you now. It's not like I haven't helped you before." He smiles mischievously, taking a longer look over my body this time, and I splutter. He certainly hasn't helped me with *that*. I stare at him in disbelief as he sinks down next to where I had been sitting at the foot of my cave.

What is he playing at?

"Hardly help. Huck would've sorted it," I grumble, taking his context an entirely a different direction. I scuff my feet at the moss growing between the rocks. As it comes loose, I kick it away, tumbling down to the ground below. He lifts an eyebrow at me, his thin lips tilted, my defiance, clearly amusing him. My cock throbs and I don't know what the fuck is wrong with me.

I hate this guy.

"Rafferty," I spin round, looking down at a man I don't recognise as he calls from below. Dressed in the same uniform as Raff, I know without a doubt, this man is one of the hunters. With serious golden eyes and a gruff voice, the man seems like he is in a hurry to get moving.

"It's my brother, I've got to go," he says. With catlike grace, he stands and stalks towards me. I go rigid, my eyes trailing his movements as comes closer. "Until next time," he whispers softly and for a moment, I think he's going to kiss me. My eyes go wide as he walks away cackling.

The fucker booped my nose.

CHAPTER 11

HUCK

Age Twenty-One

Solomon needs to grow the fuck up.

On our way back from the supply run to the outpost, the siren's loud shrieks pierced the air. Now, loaded with supplies, it's become a deadly race for us to get back to camp before the hound-like men are let loose on our trail. With Dario pinned between us, my mind can remain focused, especially as Sol's whining continues from behind.

"We could wait them out. Three against one. You ever

see the fuckers come at you more than one at a time? There's no need for this bullshit."

I take a deep breath, not letting his arrogance piss me off further than it already has. We butt heads from time to time over how to deal with the people that rule our lives. He still hasn't lost faith that someday we could leave this place. He's younger than me, and only came to the island a few years back.

This place hasn't broken him yet.

I know better.

We need to move. Get back to the safety of the caves. We were closer to the outpost than to home when the siren started and it's frustrating. My body feels like it has a constant itch beneath the skin. Taut with tension. I know it won't go until we're back. Where it is easier to keep Dario secure within our cavernous abodes.

Anything could happen out here. It's not just the ones who hunt us we need to watch out for. Other boys and men, they can be just as merciless. If not worse; we've heard the rumours.

Cannibals.

Who knows if it's true or complete bullshit? I just know I don't want to end up in someone else's belly. When the shrieking stops, I pick up my speed. The thumping footfalls and crashing of foliage is reassurance of the others behind me. None of us have the stealth to move with both speed and silence. Especially carrying such heavy packs. In this situation, it's best to just get moving.

"So now you're just ignoring me. Great," Sol huffs with annoyance. I count to ten inside my head to quell the anger. To be quite honest, I'd almost forgotten he was speaking. I was *trying* to forget. I swear he only speaks now to piss me off.

A delicate hand slips into mine. I can't help but look back into Dario's green eyes, offering him a soft smile of thanks. His comfort always offers me the strength I need and is something I cherish.

It's the most natural thing in the world for me and Dario to hold hands. I'd do anything he asked to make him happy; I even ignore my own dark desire for fear of him losing his smile. Squeezing his hand, I drag him further onwards. Ignoring the now chuckling Sol behind. He knows I'd lay down my life to protect Dario. It's why he took his place at the rear without a fuss. For that, I'll need to remember to thank him.

When we've both cooled off that is.

The heavy weight of watching eyes has my skin prickling with unease. I don't know how long we've been walking, but we still have a long way to go. I stop, raising a hand to the others and am grateful they follow my lead as they gather in closer. We all duck low. The terrain is full of shrubs and bushes, plenty enough for us to hide in. The sun is low in the sky, and it's not long until sunset. It makes vision much harder as I peer into the surrounding trees.

Tense moments pass as I stare into the surrounding area when I spot Rafferty. A hunter, and a man who should be against us, but in the past, he's helped us. His finger is to his lips. I tilt my head to him in acknowledgement.

I look at Dario and Solomon, checking that they have seen too. Both nod, though Sol's big brown eyes roll with animosity. He doesn't like the idea of Rafferty helping us. Never has. Stubborn to the core.

Howls erupt around us. I realise we've been herded in place, yet we didn't see anyone coming. My shoulders stiffen. The noise is to scare us from hiding. Dario's hand grips mine tighter, and his body trembles slightly. I know he's never fully healed from that first night out here in the woods and despite my efforts, he's always been more reserved.

Laughter and rowdy banter comes from behind us, ahead of us, everywhere, from multiple sources. It's not the predators who come after the sirens. These are some of our own. Ones who take pleasure in the hunt as much as the ones who brought us here.

Among their many crimes, they enjoy stealing, fighting and humiliating the weak. It appears they also want to give away our position to those true hunters. As they come into view, I see the multiple lines scoring their right arms. It's a mark of who they are. These are the men who claim to have devoured flesh. Today is not the day we will find out the truth of that rumour.

Rafferty lets out a piercing whistle and stands to gain the men's attention. Their raucous laughter vanishes, and heavy footsteps move in his direction. He remains still. His grey eyes are bright, his smile wide as he takes in the five men moving towards him.

"Hello. You appear to be after your injections, gentlemen. Either that or this unseemly loud behaviour is rather unnecessary." His jovial tone is ridiculous. I bite my lip to hold back the laugh while shaking my head. He has no fear, standing confidently before these men who look at him like he's nuts.

I'm pretty sure he is.

It makes me wonder if they've not encountered Rafferty before. More often than not, he's on our side of the island. They look from one to another. One of the younger men in the bunch, wiry with thick black hair, steps forward. He clicks his neck, attempting to intimidate Raff, who just fake yawns and looks at the standard watch all his fellow hounds have.

"I don't think so. We don't answer to you," the man jeers. His neck arches back, snaps forwards and spits into Raff's face. His friends laugh as a dark smile pulls at his lips. Raff swipes his black uniformed arm across his tanned cheek.

Faster than I can track, the man is on the ground, a needle pressed to his neck. Raff presses the plunger down and laughs maniacally. His smile is something out of nightmares. His teeth look elongated and are much sharper than usual. The low sun sinking to nightfall, catching his grey eyes. They almost seem to glow. The whole thing gives off a monstrous effect on someone who is a normally handsome man.

"You chaps want yours now?"

The others run.

"Oh, I do so love when they run, unfortunately today I have other business."

They leave behind their wiry brethren, who shuffles backwards away from the predator. He spins to get to his hands and knees and follows behind the others.

Me, Dario and Sol rise as one. Dario's hand still clutches tightly around my own, while Sol eyes me wearily. We cautiously make our way towards Rafferty. Though he looks much more his usual self; laughter is still very much in his voice as he speaks. I'm still not sure if he's friend or foe, but I have to keep reminding myself of the help he's given us.

"I'll escort you back. I have an idea to run by you."

I must admit, I'm intrigued by whatever he has to suggest. Looking at Solomon and Dario; I'm pretty certain they're at their limit. Before I can say anything, Sol can't help but spout his mouth off.

"Not sure I want to hear what you've got to say," he snaps. I turn to glower at the man, but he just shrugs, running a hand through his mop of curly black hair. "Don't tell me you hadn't thought of it. Not like he's going to offer us a way off the island or anything. The guy is crazy."

Finger caught up in a knot in his hair, he starts to gently pull and tease it apart. I shake my head at him. Was he starting to understand that this place really held no hope of escape, or just being an awkward bastard?

I figure it's the latter.

"Either way, Raff helped us out. We might as well hear what he's got to say." I try to make Sol see reason. Knowing that the hot-headed git knows how to listen for short periods of time. Even if he doesn't much like to.

"He's talking while you walk, it's up to you if you choose to listen to him or not," Rafferty singsongs. I chuckle at Raff's antics. Solomon's anger is palpable, his breathing increases and fury blazes in his eyes. I swear, I hear him muttering numbers under his breath. It makes a pleasant change from it being me.

"Just give us our jabs and fuck off."

Wrong answer. In a tumble of blurred movement, Raff has the taller man pinned down beneath him. Solomon is bucking, kicking, and growling fiercely; his hands restrained above his head in a tight grip. Raff straddles his waist, but Sol fights back with everything he's got.

Raff holds him steady throughout it all, with no sign of letting up. It's a losing battle and Solomon knows it as he lets out a final huff of air. He turns his head to the side in defeat as his body relaxes.

It feels like an invasion of privacy as I watch Rafferty move a hand to Sol's face, urging him to meet his eyes.

Soft words are spoken much too quietly for my ears to pick up as he caresses Sol's dark skin.

I look at Dario next to me, feeling awkward. His green eyes are taking in the scene. Small, knowing smile on his lips. I raise a brow as he turns his attention to me, and his smile grows wider, but he just shakes his head. I squeeze his hand.

"Happy?"

"Ecstatic, now get the fuck off me," Sol grumbles.

"Nope. Think I'll just stay here until what I need to say gets said."

Raff has administered Sol's injection in the brief time that I'd looked away. Now he seems reluctant to leave his cushioned seat. That, or he's determined to leave me with a pissed off Sol for eternity. Hell, it's getting to be tempting to leave Sol behind with Raff about now, if only to get some peace from what I know is going to be a headache later on.

"Raff, come on. Let the guy up. He'll listen, right Sol?" I bargain with the pair, hoping for some kind of movement soon. Letting out a grunt, Sol nods his agreement.

"Fine," Raff says, dragging the word out and rolling his mirth filled grey eyes before leaping from the other's lap. Sol sits quickly, pulling his knees up to his chest, shielding himself. I smirk knowingly at Sol, who glares daggers right back at me.

"So, I wanted to ask if you'd be interested in a mutual exchange of sorts. I already go to your end of the island— more specifically, I always head to the caves. In the future, rather than having to play tedious games of hide and seek like we always do, I'd like to propose that you come to me and my brother freely."

I take in the information he gives, nodding along as he checks his watch. Coming freely to him doesn't seem too much of a hardship. But at what cost?

"I'll be honest with you here. There are bigger players than us. I shouldn't even be telling you that. We have no control over what injections you are given; we just follow our instructions. The more we give out, the easier things are for us. You guys don't even run, just hide. It's tenuous and time consuming."

"So, what do we get out of this? Besides queuing up for you like sacrificial lambs?" Solomon grates out between clenched jaws. I must admit, so far, I can't see how this is beneficial.

"Not a lot, I know. What I can guarantee is safety from worse fates. You get your injection and whatever result the doctor wants is in their hands. You've all survived that shit before and if you're all together, you can help each other through any side effects. Well, if you can, anyway."

Raff has the decency to grimace as he explains. He pulls out the case I know to hold the vials and needles for our jabs from the jacket pocket of his uniform. Placing the black square case down, he begins sorting out what he needs. We have survived these poisons, but I've also seen many who haven't. I don't speak out my concerns, but by his continued speech, the thoughts must've been clear on my face as I watch him.

"I don't know if you've met my psychotic brother. He's the kind of man you don't survive. Him and the men from earlier are what I'll be keeping you from. Devon has taken it upon himself to team up with that little gang of monsters. What they leave behind... let's just say, it's not pretty."

I didn't know the name of the black-eyed demon that roamed this island when the siren rang. His tendencies and preferences to maiming were legendary, though. The stone dagger tucked into my pocket was a powerful reminder of why I never went unarmed. Because of that very man.

"Who is the brother you want to bring with you then?" Dario speaks up, his curiosity piqued. Pulling away from me, he allows Raff to apply his jab with no fuss. I walk up behind to get my own, noting the difference in colours between our two vials.

"He's good, even compared to me. You can trust him. He needs this. I worry about him and what they will do to him if his numbers don't increase. He's not a natural hunter like me."

The intrusion of the needle is so familiar, I don't flinch as the cold liquid filters into my veins. Thinking it over, either way they make us have this toxin put into our veins. Not having to run or hide can only be a good thing. If Rafferty can keep even the worst of the others away, it might be worth it. I look at Dario.

It'll be worth it.

"Okay. You stop your men and any others on this

island being a problem when you're here. Then you and your brother will have access to as many at the caves who agree. I will speak to them in the morning after we arrive home. To be honest, I don't think it'll be much of an issue."

"You can't be serious," Sol seethes, rising to his feet and storming his way over to us. His booming voice by me is overly loud. My ears begin to vibrate and light dances across my eyes.

"I only said those who agree, Sol. You don't have to." It's hard to answer while I'm so nauseous. Not realising, Sol glares at us both, fury shining in his eyes.

"I'll see you next siren, Solomon," Rafferty teases, his voice smug.

I ignore the pair as they banter back and forth, not able to take it any longer. I rub my aching temples and fear this is an oncoming migraine. With this unending swirling in my gut, I just hope it's nothing induced by the damn injection.

We need to get home.

Dario gives me a worried look; I hadn't even noticed I'd released my hand from his to massage my head. I give him a fond smile as I retake his hand. His red hair flops into his eyes and I swear he did it purposefully to hide the tension there. He knows me just as well as I know him. Our tension has always been something we shared, and he can tell something is not right with me. Right now, all my focus needs to be on getting us back.

"Fuck off out of here. You've got your way, but don't

expect to see me there," Sol barks out, and attempts to shove the man. Raff barks a laugh.

"Toodles," Raff chuckles, lifting his hand and wiggles his fingers in a small wave. His grin full of shining white teeth, before he turns and jogs away from us. Solomon glares daggers at his retreating back, and I know the rest of this journey is going to be heaps of fun with his stroppy arse.

A tingle, a buzz and then scorching heat radiates through my head. I sink to my knees, pulling my head into my hands in pain. I hear nothing, see nothing, but the excruciating agony of a thousand red-hot pokers swirling inside my brain. It is unbearable.

It's not long before it eases off. Dario sits across from me; his soft hands caress my cheeks. Wiping away the tears I didn't know had fallen. Solomon stands tall above us, his watchful eye searching the forest.

From the distance is Rafferty's echoing laughter. As if he found amusement in what just happened. I always knew the guy was mad, but this maniacal cackling is a tad bizarre, even for him. Maybe Sol was right, and we shouldn't trust him. That's when the crazy one's voice filters into my head. My eyes widen in shock.

Enjoy the ride, Huck.

Fuck, this is new.

If I'm hearing voices, perhaps it's me who's the crazy one.

Solomon: *I can't believe he's letting that arrogant twat do this. We'll all be dead before the next siren ends. He'll see I'm right. It can't happen. I won't let it happen. Not to me. I can't submit to him.*

I let Sol brood in silence, but I can't stop his thoughts from penetrating my head as we walk the last stretch home. My head is ready to explode, pulse pounding as his words spin round my brain. Not the full migraine, but possibly worse with this side order of spewing thoughts. I know if he doesn't figure his shit out, he'll blow. So better this, than the implosion that Sol could be.

The power of mind reading. Not as great as people might like to think. The other two have shown no sign of symptoms yet, but that doesn't always mean anything. Sometimes it takes a few hours to kick in. Not this though. This is front and centre with no way to block the consistent noise out.

I haven't told them; I am embarrassed. To be inside their personal thoughts and invade their privacy is a violation. Not wanting them to run from me, I try every-thing to not listen, to not hear, as words sink inside, but it is impossible. I couldn't bear to be alone. So, I remain silent, even as every thought filters into me.

Solomon: *I can't believe how easily he pinned me down. I need to get stronger.*

Dario: *Rafferty and Solomon, a very interesting combo.*

Keeping my face impassive as Dario's thoughts penetrate my mind is unbearable. Fucking Rafferty knew exactly what I was getting into with this one tonight. I hope like hell this doesn't last long.

Dario: *Is Huck okay? He looks so stressed.*

Solomon: *The twat as good as assaulted me tonight. Why can't they see he's bad news? Who does that? He's not normal. He's a manipulator. That's what he is.*

Dario: *It's such a big decision. I'm not sure this is a good idea.*

Solomon: *He's a liar.*

Dario: *Then again, we can't know without trying.*

Solomon: *He's a manipulator.*

Dario: *And Rafferty is more trustworthy than most.*

My shoulders relax at the sight of the caves. I won't have to take in much more of this. This constant barrage of competing thoughts all the time is enough to drive me completely insane.

Solomon: *He's going to kill us all.*

"Raff is going to get us all killed," Sol speaks his thoughts at last, but I have to shut him down. I've listened to his ranting for miles. I'm not listening to the encore of his mind out loud.

"The deal is done; I'll talk to the others in the morning. I'm certain they'll all agree. Now, I'm completely beat and it's time for bed. Goodnight." My words are short but final as I walk out from the trees towards the rock formation that holds our cave utopia. I hold back the grin as I hear his unspoken parting shot not meant for my ears.

Solomon: *Fucking prick.*

I pull Dario up the couple of steps to our level of the cave and, as always, he stumbles into me. I wrap my arms around him like I did that first night, and I rest my head atop of his.

It feels so good when he holds me like this.

I pull away from him; it's like I'm taking advantage of him and his thoughts if I continued. Unable to help myself, my smile is wide as he takes my hand to walk. This has always been our way. Part of our natural connection to one another.

I pretend not to hear his thoughts in my head. I can't let myself listen to things that are not spoken out loud. Not wanting to cross a barrier, I know he would never accept. It only gets worse as I hear his panted groans later that night. Knowing he's so close, allowing himself the pleasure I can only dream of giving him.

Yes, fuck yes. Huck. Please.

I palm my erection, squeezing it and trying not to moan or move. Not to catch Dario's attention. Listening to his thoughts, as his pants become little whines of pleasure, makes it difficult to stay impassive. Even this is wrong, but a man can only be good for so long with such a temptation. He thinks I'm asleep. Normally, I'm a deep sleeper, and it makes me question just how often Dario pleasures himself as I lay so close by. Thinking of me.

Shit, I'm coming. Fuck. So good. Huck.

My name in his thoughts as he cries out his release is a heady emotion. I experience a taste of power, despite doing nothing. Slurping noises echo the cave walls, and my eyes go wide. Just moving my eyes, I can just make out Dario licking his fingers clean from the glow of the fire.

Fuck. My dick twitches and I can't help but wish that was my cum he was sucking from his fingers. The perfect picture of purity tasting his own cum like a cum-guzzling little slut. I'm tempted to 'wake up' and watch that sweet blush taint his cheeks. Realising how close he had been to being caught, not knowing the reality of his voyeur.

Of course, that's when he snuggles back down into his sleeping bag. Wriggling down like he always does, his pert arse tauntingly poised in my direction.

Hell, I want him.

I bite my lip. It's not like I've never thought about it. Fuck, it's been in my dreams for years. Of taking his lush lips with mine. Of threading my thick, aching cock inside his wanting mouth. I want to bend him over, ease inside him nice and slow. Yes, it's definitely played in my mind. On repeat, as desire and fantasy collide.

The problem is, I'd destroy him.

I don't just want him to suck my cock. I want to fuck his mouth until he's gagging on me. I want his tears trailing down his perfect face as he's unable to breathe. When I pound into his tight little ring, I want to pull on his hair, bite him, spank him in an act of outright dominance.

I need him to be mine.

I need to make him submit.

I need to *own him* completely.

Yet, he is the only thing keeping my heart beating. Does that mean he really owns me?

He's so soft, sweet, and innocent. I love him. I know I do. He's my best friend, but he's so much more to me than that. I know part of him must feel the same way. There's attraction and fondness. I can't tell him though. What would I do if he ever found out what went on inside my head, what I wanted from him?

What I need.

If he rejected me. I don't think I could handle it. I would never fully recover, and it petrifies me.

I would be lost without him.

So, instead of giving in to my forbidden desires, I do nothing, ensuring I won't jeopardise what we already have.

CHAPTER 12

NIXI

Age Seventeen

I don't let my mind wander to Alice back at camp. I need to remain focused on myself. My feet slip on the uneven ground beneath me. The downpour from this morning causes issues to my usual tactics. The muddied ground dried just enough to reveal my footprints. I curse.

I'm not far enough, when the empty silence takes over from the call of the siren. It's a sign for the hunt to begin. Like wraiths, they come, and they take, only giving us suffering in return. Too soon, the screams of my camp mates echo into the night. I can't let myself stop. I need to find safety in the wooded landscape before I can think of rest.

My heart pounds erratically, like it always does. Fear consumes me; maybe this time it won't be him. My grey eyed stalker that hunts me relentlessly. I know I should fear him too, but I don't.

Even with him, I fight.

Despite his kinder nature, he still injects me with poison. I've seen what it can do. So far, I've been lucky. But in the back of my mind, a whispered voice insists it's not luck at all. Maybe my persistent predator has a hand in that too.

He calls me Wildcat.

I shake away the thoughts. I can't focus on him right now. A scream to my right pulls my concentration. Too late, I look ahead to slam into a large tree and my head crashes into a low-hanging branch. That'll teach me to go off the pathways. A drip rolls down my temple and I swipe it away with the back of my hand.

Blood.

I turn around too fast, making my head spin. I lean up against the trunk of the tree and slip slowly to the ground. The grinding press of the bark scratches up my back. I take deep, steadying breaths as I try to control the whirlpool in my head. One look at my palms and I can see they took most of the impact. They're both scraped up to pieces. I was running too fast. I don't know if I'm even going to be able to walk right now, let alone run. Hell, standing could be interesting.

Shit, this is bad.

I don't let myself go back to that time often, a time when I was a scared little girl. Without knowledge or power to even try to attempt fighting back. It's futile; they always win in the end. I never give up though. I never let them have the satisfaction of my tears. Not anymore.

Right now though, I feel it. Deep in my bones, I feel myself surrender to my younger self. I watch with frightened eyes as I pull myself tightly against the tree, wishing to be invisible. A dark laugh ripping from me at the thought that one of their shots can do just that.

These men, these predators, can scent blood in the air. It's only a matter of time. My stalker won't be interested if there's no game to play. He won't protect me tonight.

A woman comes stumbling past, not even glancing in my direction. Her dress torn, exposing her breasts, but her cries are silent.

Soon that will be me.

I'm startled as a belch erupts from her mouth. Her eyes widen in panic as she collapses to the floor on her knees. She starts to gag and retch with her hand across her mouth. I'm mere metres from her, but she still doesn't notice me. I don't know if I should help, or if I should leave her to her misery.

She cries out in pain from her first bout of sickness. I crawl dizzily to her side. For the first time I realise it's one of Aggs' friends, Katie. I place a cool hand on her forehead. It's scalding to the touch; something is far from right. Too weak to protest, she allows me to pull back her hair as best I can as she vomits again. It doesn't matter as bile splatters my legs. It will wash.

Her stomach makes a gurgle and Katie pales. The acrid scent surrounding us now joined with the pungent smell of her bowels letting loose. Her cries turn into pained whimpers, and she curls up into herself on the filth covered muddy ground.

I don't know what to do.

I instantly regret swinging my head round at the swishing of foliage. My vision swims and I grip my head, closing my eyes tightly. I vaguely recall it being similar to a fairground ride I'd once been on. Me and my best friend had been so excited that it was close enough to walk to from the foster home. I can barely remember Zee's face now.

"Wildcat," his voice calls softly to me. I open my eyes, slowly peering at him as he edges ever closer. Knowing now it's my grey-eyed stalker, my shoulders relax ever so slightly. I turn my body towards him, shielding Katie behind me.

I know he made the noise on purpose. It's all part of the game we play. What I don't understand is why he's still playing. I'm not alone. I'm injured and have barely gone far enough to sate his hunger for the hunt.

"You win."

He has the nerve to scoff, as if my words mean nothing to him. Perhaps this time they don't. It hasn't been much of a competition to win after all.

"You're injured." His voice is annoyed and my eyes

narrow. I'm more than aware of my own failings, but it's not me I'm worried about right now. My hand moves protectively to Katie's back with my eyes remaining locked on his.

"Help her."

"I can't do that, Wildcat."

"Why not?" This is the most I've ever spoken to him. My need to help her outweighs the fight within me. I don't understand why these men do this to us. Use us the way they do. For what purpose could they possibly have to keep us here other than their sick perversions?

"It's against the rules."

It's my turn to scoff. Whose rules? These men make the damn rules.

"She needs help, please," I beg. My heart sinks, and I try a different tactic. The desperation is thick in my voice, I am not willing to leave her here alone. I don't care if others wouldn't do the same for me. Her little whines combined with her trembling body behind me make me realise I could never forgive myself if I left her here.

"Please. I'll do anything you ask."

His body tenses, eyes flicking away briefly from mine.

"I'll take her back to your camp. It's the best I can offer. First you need your injection, it'll..." He pauses in thought. "Dissuade the others." He's blunt, and I wince. I know he's not wrong. That once that toxin gets into your bloodstream, the men lose interest.

"I can walk with you. You can give me mine once she's back at camp."

"Last offer, Wildcat. Take it now, or leave her here," his smile is smug. I want to wipe it right off his face. He knew the instant the words left my mouth that I had no hope in hell. I won't be walking anywhere right now.

"You win."

My repeated words are not lost on him as his brow raises. I look back towards the girl, unable to linger in his gaze a moment longer. Without thinking, I rub small circles on Katie's back. His victory is worth her safety. Her shuddering breaths not quite covering the sounds of his purposeful booted footsteps walking ever closer.

The prick of the needle is barely noticeable. I had almost hoped he wouldn't go through with it, and that this time, things would be different. They never are; it's always the same.

Maybe this time, at least, I'll get something of use. Strength perhaps, the last time I'd had that it had lasted for days. As a yawn escapes me, I glare at the man, who now steps around me. So much for safety.

My grey eyed stalker pays me no mind as he crouches down to the woman. To him, it doesn't matter that I'm angry at his choices. He is in charge here. He frowns as he rests a hand on her forehead, his eyes finally meeting mine.

"I'll take her now. I'll be back for you, Wildcat."

Cradling her lightly, he doesn't even wince as he lifts her smoothly to his chest. Completely unbothered by the smell now permeating her body, he rises to his feet. No doubt in the direction he turns. Walking at a steady pace, he leaves me behind.

Another yawn breaching my lips. I don't want to be left vulnerable out here. Desperately, I try to keep my eyes open while watching the pair grow smaller in the distance. Nearly out of sight, he looks back at me, tipping his head. Before disappearing into the trees with the woman in his arms.

My eyes drift closed, and I remember no more.

I didn't let it bother me; I'd known a hunter would catch me last night as I held her hair. That by tomorrow, she would probably hate me as I begged for him to take her back to camp. Never crossed my mind that they had given her one of their foul experiments.

I was just a person, helping another in pain.

Katie died last night.

Defiled, ruined, and in unimaginable torment. I hadn't even made it back to camp myself before her life slipped away. Then again, even if I had, I wouldn't have been awake.

Like Katie before me, he carried me back to camp, settling me back in my makeshift tomb of a home. The fact he knew exactly which of them is mine is a worry for another day, as I recall the poor broken woman who passed away in the night.

As Katie lay under the stars, the few friends that still remained in camp gathered round her. They held her hand and whispered all the words I didn't have to give. It's more than most of us get. I didn't help her for recognition. I thought she would live. Still, she wanted a message to be passed on; to thank me for not leaving her behind, to die alone. To thank me for my kindness, for stopping.

For bringing her home.

To her family.

CHAPTER 13

SOLOMON

Age Twenty

I speed through the trees. Branches and leaves whip at my body, but I don't care. I'll never let the fuckers take me easily. Evergreens, autumn yellows, browns, reds, and oranges flash past my vision, blurring like a memory just out of my periphery. The siren blasted only minutes ago; I know I have to find somewhere safe to secure myself. To fight the bastards who want to harm me.

The biggest bastard of them all is that fucker Rafferty —the one who has them all fooled into submission. I will never bow down to them. Raff has them all lining up, like good little puppets taking the needle into their necks without complaint. Doesn't matter that the poison sliding into their bloodstream could kill them. To them, he's saving them. He's making sure the bigger, badder men don't hurt them. HA. He's manipulated them. He is the worst of them all.

"I'm not here to hurt you."

Those whispered words while he caressed my face. His grey eyes staring deeply into mine, urging me to trust him. The memory still haunts me. Clouds my thoughts. Messes with my judgments.

I won't be made a fool of.

It's been months since he made that agreement. Maybe even a year. I've had no problems doing things the way I always have. I've not run into a bigger monster. The only one I see hides behind a manic smile and goes to my camp, gaining power from their compliance.

Hidden amongst the rocks above, I stayed to watch the first time they accepted the needle willingly. I stared down at my people as they stood in line. Saw for myself, the *saviour* at work. I watched a man get injected by Rafferty. Barely seconds later, the effects activated. His skin started to ripple and crack as sweat beaded at his temple. His mouth tearing open on a scream.

His so-called friends all stepped away from him.

The man had been one of the eldest on the island—in his thirties. He had possibly even been the one who'd found the damn caves our group sheltered in. It didn't matter, these little mice were all moving away. It was as if he meant absolutely nothing to them. They dared not get any closer to whatever fate beheld him.

Well, except for our hero Huck, of course. I'd watched on as Huck pushed through the gathered crowd. Dario close behind. Raff and his brother held their arms out firm stopping the pair from getting any closer. As if they knew exactly what was to come.

Of course they had. They'd seen this before.

They'd done this before.

I knew I was right not to trust them. Glad I hadn't given in so easily. The man exploded like the trick birthday cake my uncle once gave me—a cake that had sent my parents into a tailspin. He'd disintegrated into unrecognisable chunks of bloodied flesh. Blood pooling into the dry mud. I felt sickened by the sight. I can now relate to how that cake had given my parents flashbacks with hunks of thick jam oozing onto the floor in a steady drip.

Rafferty was nothing but a snake, one who was to tempt us with the fruit of corruption. I was not one to fall for his calculated lies and deception. I would not follow in the wake of my brainwashed camp.

Even as I watched on, my group moved towards him. They step through the blood of their fallen to willingly take the injection. It stained their feet red. Huck and Dario look on; their faces dappled in flecks of gore, as one by one, our camp mates took their jabs. There wasn't a hint of reluctance despite their possible fate. It disturbed me more than I could ever describe.

I would not become like that man who had been violently ripped from this world. Trampled over upon his death. There hadn't even been enough pieces of him left to bury.

That would not be me.

I didn't need to witness more after that. Leaving camp, I caught Rafferty's grey eyes. It didn't matter that he looked tired, or that as I passed, he cast a worried look at his golden-eyed brother. All I could think about was getting away from the horror show that I'd just witnessed.

I've avoided Raff since. Any time I caught a hint of him being in the area, I've hidden. It may be childish, but the man has destroyed what we once had here. People are forgetting exactly who he is to us. He is the enemy, and if we give into him, we have no hope of freedom. At least I know, when the sirens ring, what I have to do. What I always did before.

I have to run.

Run and fight.

I will not give in; I will not give up.

The blow to the back of my head comes from nowhere.

I'd heard nothing, seen nothing. Like a phantom raised

itself from a void of nothingness to strike me down. I keep my footing despite my fast pace, whirling and trying to ignore the dizziness as lights flash in my vision. Pain splinters through my skull.

As I make out my attacker, his sinister grin and black eyes brings bile to my throat. This man is the one who Raff was truly offering his protection from. Rafferty may be the manipulative snake, but this one doesn't hide his taint. The brother, Devon.

There're many forms of monster in this world and Devon is the kind who hides under your bed, scratching at the underside of it as you tremble beneath your blankets. He's the kind of demon who loves for you to become powerless as you try to fight him. For him to break and ruin you.

To destroy you.

I take a step backwards, then another, and another. His smile only grows larger, eyes darkening with the thrill for the hunt, the chase. Like a cat playing with a mouse, he has me exactly where he wants. My head pounds, swirling confusion as I try to think. Nothing is clear, all I that comes to me is—*not him.*

Anyone but him.

Even Rafferty and his manipulations are better than this.

Damn my stubborn arse.

Hindsight is a fucking bitch. I can't change anything now as he inches forward. His foot falls impossibly silent on the leaf strewn ground. I match him step for step, but he's on me before I even fully turn. He staunches my attempt to run before I ever had the chance.

I should have known this monster would never let its prey escape. My aching head crashes into the muddied ground, but I can't let the pain phase me as the man atop me cackles. I kick my legs out and try to turn to gain any purchase. My goal is to stand, but my feet slip in the squelching mud. Rainfall has been upon us for weeks and the result is destroying any hope of my escape.

A piercing pain tears into my side like sharp claws, straight through my clothes into my flesh. He must have a weapon. I have nothing to fight him back with. I can't even get to my damn feet. Another stab has me letting out a startled yell. The flashing light and darkness contorting my vision makes me realise that the hit to my head may have caused a concussion. My mind whirls with agony and hopelessness. Laughter roars through my ears as this monster enjoys his tormenting game.

He leans further over my frame, his body a tonne of bricks, crushing my battered one. His weight pinning me down easily, despite my desperate struggles. He leans on one elbow, staring at my face, his eyes as dark as pitch. Soulless. My body stills as he rocks his groin against me. Devon smirks, knowing I feel the hardness of him rubbing against me.

"You're not as pretty as some others. There's one little delicacy I would really like to sample. He keeps evading me, has his bodyguard protecting him. I'm a simple creature. I'll fuck anything really. So long as they hurt. As long as they bleed."

His fingers caress my face, and I let out a shuddering breath. It's too similar to his touch. He bends down, his lips touch my ear, his whispers.

"You know what's most fun. When I see the light in their eyes fade to nothing as I pound my release into their bodies. Nothing is as powerful as that. If only I was allowed off my leash more often."

I want to vomit, but I won't give him the satisfaction. Already he's told me something he probably shouldn't. Devon's not allowed to kill me. Whatever happens tonight —and at this point, I know something will happen—whatever despicable, insidious thing he does to me, I will live. I just need to stay in one piece.

I don't make a move, don't even blink. Maybe that is what enrages the demon? Letting out a snarl, he grabs hold of my lengthy hair, long fallen from its tie. Viciously, he pulls my head up, then slams it down repeatedly into the dirt beneath us. The squish of the mud cushioning the blows. It's not enough to sate his frustration as he stands, lifting me by my hair. I slip in the mud, trying to get to my feet, feeling the tugging sensation of my hair being ripped out from the roots.

I twist, pulling and kicking out at him, freeing myself. I flee, ignoring the chunk of hair ripped from my scalp. Desperate and fast, I go, knowing it's futile. But I have to try all the same. Caked in mud, blood still pouring from my injuries, and the swirling concussion clawing at my head from multiple blows, I run on.

Smacking into a pillar of stone, one that grips my arms like vices. How the fuck did he get ahead of me? A shove pushes me back to the floor. I crash back onto my side, wincing at the pain from the tearing wound there. I shut my eyes briefly, squeezing them, before I rip them back open. Desperately trying to orientate myself.

His booted feet walk calmly towards me, and I try not to let the wrenching agony I'm in deter me. I need to stay strong. As he walks with slow, torturous steps, I must pass out for a second. I don't see the kick that comes swiftly smashing into my face. Blood gushes down my nose, the echoing crack shuddering through my ears. I shakily raise my arms to cover my face against another blow, curling my body up as small as possible. Against the volley of kicks thrown at me, it's not any kind of protection.

I'm weak, pathetic. Snot and blood oozes down my face as I let out howling cries of agony. It's not until he speaks that I know a dark, cunning saviour has come for me.

"That's one of my group, Devon. Leave him be." I didn't think I'd ever be happy to hear that conniving bastard. Yet, I don't know if I'll be alive after tonight if I stay with this man. No matter what leash he's supposed to be on.

"Beat it, Rafferty. It's my plaything for today."

He kicks me in the ribs once more. I try to keep my eyes open as I cough violently, my chest aching. That time might have a broken rib; shit, I hope it's not a punctured lung. I give in, closing my eyes even tighter than before, clenching my teeth against the writhing pain, unable to focus on little else. A growl penetrates the air. Much more beastly than man, I try to look but find I can't.

Violence permeates the air, the sound guttural and tearing, but all too soon I'm lost to the darkness of my mind.

I awaken to a fire blazing, my body roaring out as much as the embers. Every part of me aches. I suppose this is karma for believing I could do this alone. The dancing flames burn away the darkness surrounding us. Me and the man who saved me, the one I owe my life to, the one I've always hated with a scorching fury.

From the other side of the fire, Rafferty watches me with his head tilted to one side like a damn dog. His expression is almost curious as our eyes meet. I'm the first to look away. Guilt gnawing at me for thinking the worst of him. He owes me nothing, yet still, he came and saved me.

It makes me wonder what kind of life he'd had growing up, to decide he has to help us. Maybe he's not the snake after all, or perhaps he still is. I just forget about the devil who puts that snake on his path.

I groan as I try to sit, my every muscle and bone protesting at the movement. Immediately, he's by my side, pressing gently on my shoulder to make me lie back down. I'm so weakened, I can't even push against him.

"You need rest. Go back to sleep, I'll get you back to camp in the morning," his words are less scornful than I had expected, his tone almost void of all emotion. I know he's right, but I don't want to rest when he's here. Despite him helping me tonight, it still could be a play he's trying. Then again, my head is so muddled. Shit, should I be sleeping if I have a concussion anyway?

"I need a drink. Can't do that on my back. Plus, pretty sure I'm concussed and shouldn't be sleeping." I can't seem to shut my mouth. It must break something in him too, at the exasperated look he gives me; his grey eyes are full of frustration as he drags a hand through his shaggy hair.

"Look, kid," Raff growls. Who the fuck is he calling a kid? We must be the same age, a year's difference at most. He shuffles closer, raising my head as carefully as possible to his knees, a canteen in hand. He tips water into my mouth a little at a time as he speaks. "I checked you over. You're not showing any symptoms of a serious head injury. You may have a concussion, but you're okay to rest up and sleep. I've cleaned you up best I can, but I don't have any bandages. I got you into shelter so you can rest. Now get to sleep so I don't have to carry your stubborn arse the entire way back tomorrow because you're too physically exhausted to do so."

I notice for the first time his torn t-shirt showing under his open uniform jacket, long strips of missing material. He must've used that to both bandage and clean me up. The cloying mud I'd been covered with is no longer coating my skin.

Looking around, we're in an unfamiliar cave and it almost makes me laugh. As a kid, I would've thought they all looked the same, but not anymore. As gently as he did before, he cradles my head back to the ground, my thirst quenched.

"Solomon, my name is Solomon."

"I know what your name is," he says. A sly grin quirks up at the edges of his mouth. "Kid. Now sleep, please." I try not to chuckle at the dick, but it's exactly the sort of thing I would have said in his position. I give a slight nod, finally giving into his demands. He obviously isn't trying to cause me any additional harm. I can only truly be grateful for what he's done tonight.

"Thanks, Raff," I murmur as I shut my eyes. I don't hear him reply, if he does, as sleep claims me.

My dreams are wild, full of chaos and unbridled pain.

Flashes of howling, beastly laughter crashes through my nightmares. Person after person takes injection after injection. Their bodies succumb to death in different, volatile, and disturbing ways. A mass grave fills with the flesh, blood and bones of all the victims of this heinous society we can never escape.

I run through a labyrinth of never-ending woodland. Going nowhere and always circling back to where I started.

A cool palm of a hand presses against my forehead. It pushes me back into the sinking mud beneath me and I'm drowning. Every crevice of my body fills with the syrupy sludge, talons wrapping round my sides that tear into me from beneath. Dragging me further below into the murky depths of nothingness.

I try to rip my eyes open, to free myself from the torment, only to see Rafferty lit up with firelight. A needle is in his hand, injecting the poison into himself. I swear, I can see as the tendrils of blackness creep through his veins. Another type of monster coiling and clawing at him, devouring him from the inside. My vision wavers, darkness colliding into me and in a blink, he's there, in front of me, with whispered words I can't hear.

I scream, the sound silent to my ears. The terror within me is unlike anything I've experienced. Is this nightmare a reality or am I still inside my head, filled with demon-like dreams?

Calloused hands soothingly trail through my hair, across my cheeks, wiping away the tears I don't realise

I've shed. His head lies next to mine and our breathing syncs in time as one. As once more I am sinking into the floor beneath me.

This time, I am not alone as the darkness of the world pulls me under, down and still further down. Arms curl around my waist protectively, gently with utmost care, they never leave me. Not until the morning light comes around and it's time to painfully go home.

I never did take the injection that night. He knew I had been too weak to survive it. The next time the sirens called, I was the first in line for my injection and every time after that.

Running and fighting, after all, had been my worst mistake.

It had been a fool's game all along.

CHAPTER 14

NIXI

Age Twenty-One

I haven't gotten far enough. I left it too late to run. Multiple sets of boots thud behind me as I flee. I haven't felt this vulnerable in years. I don't even dare to look over my shoulder as I speed through trees. Greenery and flowers flashing past my vision in a blur of colour.

My heart feels as though it will beat right out of my chest any second as my footsteps pound the floor, dry earth kicking up behind me. I can't stop, won't stop, not until I'm far enough away to hide from these hunters, these monsters, these demons in the night. I won't let their vile touches taint my skin like they have so many years before.

I can't let it happen again.

Hands catch hold of my dress as I run, tearing the fabric in their clasp. They're too quick, too close. They've always been too fast, it's not normal. I push myself harder, but I stumble; my logic leaving me as fear ratchets up. Momentum moving me forward but slower than I need. Fingers twist through my hair and a scream rips out of me as I am forced backwards. My world blurs with intense motion.

Bile reaches my throat as I see who has me caught in his grasp. This creature has haunted my nightmares for years. With eyes that are soulless depths of pitch black and hair to match, he is the epitome of a demon. He holds no interest in my comfort as he uses his grip in my curls to force me down, crashing onto my knees.

Another body collides into him, and he lashes out with one hand at his attacker, while keeping me in place. Two dogs clawing over a bone, a toy, a treat, or in this case, me. They both war to burn in the pits of hell, but perhaps we are already there. I don't know what I did wrong, but maybe I am the reward for the devil's children.

"She's mine tonight."

"I've waited too long to fuck this tight cunt again."

"You'll break her."

"I'll let you use her mouth, then give you the leftovers."

The laughter as they agree upon sharing my broken body sickens me. I barely take in their words as they continue their bantering back and forth. My world turns into a haze of memories thrust to the forefront of my chaotic mind.

I can't breathe, can't think, can't move as anxiety floods through my body. Where is he? Where is my predator? Taking in a choked breath to ease my panic only helps me slightly. I've taken advantage of his protection for too long and now I need to remember how to fight. I'm not a little girl anymore.

I try to crawl from the pair, yelping out in pain as my captor yanks me back towards him. The momentum flinging me to the floor and crashing my head against the solid ground beneath. I spin to look back, unsteady, but determined, as I stare up at the two men. One still gripping a lump of my tangled hair within his grip.

I try to scramble away from them, but a large, booted foot kicks me in the stomach. My heartbeat thunders in my ears and my head throbs. Liquid, most likely blood, trails down the side of my face and know this fate is unavoidable.

I try to go into the depths of my mind, something I used to do with ease as a kid, but I am out of practice. I close my eyes, screwing them shut, willing myself away to anywhere else. To disassociate from what's to come.

I hear a roar, a loud deafening noise that makes me cover my ears. I curl into a small ball, arms and hands covering my eyes and ears as much as possible. Howl's start to break out and my body quakes, this makes no sense.

Then it's *his* voice I'm hearing, telling me to stay down. I dare not open my eyes. Is this real, or is my mind playing tricks? I'm too scared to find out. My mind can't have snapped. This must be the injection. A breeze of their moving forms shifts around me, while their words are growled unintelligibly.

By the time I finally convince myself to open my eyes, no one is here. The snarling growls echoing in the distance. I don't understand exactly what is going on, but I know my protector has come. I stare toward the noise, waiting for what comes next. Hoping that this fear is not my mind breaking.

As the silence falls, I watch with bated breath, hopeful that he has won. My heart pattering a desperate rhythm, willing him to come back to me. I could have run from him, should have run, but find myself unable to. I need to know.

I squint my eyes as a figure comes back into the silvery moonlight towards me. His silent footsteps give me hope. No one is as quiet as my predator. Closer and closer he comes until his gorgeous features are finally revealed.

Relief sinks into me that I am no longer alone in this. Despite the guilt of the other women not having this same advantage, I am relieved to have him. It was hard enough being on this island, but if I hadn't had him, I'm not sure I would have survived it all these years.

My protector, with his strong-muscled body and lithe movements that I could imagine turning into the most stunning of dances. His advances are a graceful performance, moving so deftly through the trees towards me. Only for a moment, I forget the hunter he is as I watch him approach. Never could I imagine his next move to be so forceful.

"Never leave it that late to run again, Wildcat. That was too close. You run and I will always find you."

Silver grey eyes gleam at me wickedly as he slams my body back into the tree behind me. A thrill rushes through me as the bite of the bark digs into my skin. It hurts, but I don't care as I let out panting breaths of air. My predator has saved me from the other wraiths once more and now he is here.

"What happened back there?" I ask in a breathless whisper.

"It's not time yet, Wildcat. Soon though."

The side of himself that loved to hunt me down, to have me as his prey was in charge and ready to take his prize. He moves in close, pinning me to the trunk with his body. I feel his hard length press against my stomach, and I know things will never be the same again after tonight.

His fingers swipe over the lingering wetness tracking down my face. Pulling his hand back, my blood slick on his digits, he places them on his tongue, his eyes never leaving mine. He sucks them into his mouth, cheeks hollowing, he wraps his sinister lips around them. A rumbling sounds from deep within his chest, satisfaction shining bright in his eyes. I should be horrified, but I'm not. I'm fascinated by him, like I always have been.

His smirk hypnotises me, leaving me still, even as his

huge palm wraps around my neck. A subtle caress of his thumb along my pulse has my already erratic heart skipping a beat. My eyes fall closed as a whimper escapes my lips.

His lips touch my forehead. Whisper soft kisses trailing across to the slight cut that has blood dribbling down my face. I should have expected it, something like that from him, but I flinch, jumping slightly as his tongue laps at my injury. It's a strange sensation.

My predator has never held me so close before, and it's a heady feeling that I never want to let go. Without thought, I bite my bottom lip; his other hand is there, pulling it from between my teeth before I even register it.

"These lips are only for me to bite."

My eyes open, staring upwards; he looks back down at me. Eyes a sparkling silver shining in the moonlit night. A mischievous smirk tilts his blood covered, thin lips as he ducks his head in towards me. Teeth nip at my ear, and I can't deny the aching pressure only this man has ever achieved before, a shiver ripping its way up my spine.

"In fact, I think all of you is mine for the taking."

Years of being chased by him and never touched has made me go crazy. Perhaps I don't care. For him, I have become immune to the fear instinct tells me I should be consumed by. I will always be wary of his reasoning. After all, he still injects me with poison. I will always fight him on that, but this, right here. This is something I can't seem to fight any longer.

"Wildcat," his voice is a hushed growl against my neck,

before he lays nipping kisses across my jaw, forcing my thoughts back, helping me stay in the now. "I need you to listen very carefully. I'm about to let you go, and when I do, you better not run. If you run, I will chase you down. If I chase you down, Little Seductress, you know I will catch you and when I do, 1 will fuck that dripping wet little pussy of yours." His hand squeezes briefly around my neck, looking me directly in the eye.

"Do you understand me, Little Seductress?"

I nod because I do understand, my body trembling. This is my out, the chance to stop this sizzling energy burning between us. This new dynamic is something explosive and exhilarating. I clench my thighs together; already knowing I'm going to regret my decision as soon as I make it.

I already know I am going to run, and so does he.

If anyone asks me, I'll blame the head injury. I shouldn't want this after coming so close to hell today, but I need to forget. I need to let go of the fear of my nightmares and do something for me. As he releases me, I stare into his eyes for only a second.

Without giving it another moment's thought, I run.

I don't hear his following footsteps, then again, I hadn't expected to. For the first time in years, I let loose the wildness inside me, laughing instead of concerning myself with the intense sense of fear as I race away. It's wild and thrilling. I slow my pace to briefly to peer into the woodland behind, seeing nothing.

I half expect to see him ahead of me as I turn back, but

he's nowhere to be seen as I keep moving. I know this place like the back of my hand, our very own wilderness playground to live in. For once, I am happy to be his prey.

Soon, though, the fun starts to wane as the doubts return in anxious waves. The darkness has always shrouded this place with a cloud of menace. Hiding even the moon's light with a canopy of trees and, as time continues on, dread peaks its ugly head. Telling me that things haven't gone according to plan.

I slow to a stop, my mouth dry with thirst, tension rising within me. Could they have attacked my protector? Revenge from his fellow hunters for stopping them earlier tonight? Am I out here alone, once again unprotected? My thoughts a hectic muddle inside my head as I tiredly look for somewhere to hide.

A hand reaches over my mouth, my startled cry captured as I begin to struggle. An arm locks around my waist, keeping me pinned tightly against their powerful chest. I kick my legs out, hoping to unbalance them, but it's useless. They are an immovable force.

"I told you, if you ran, I would always find you."

His dark laughter sparks electric pulses thrumming through my veins. Anticipation for what is about to happen, on my own terms. Seeking my pleasure from the violence has me giddy as desire overtakes my body.

His hard cock digs into my lower back; his hot body is plastered against me. I let out a little whimper and his menacing chuckle has me melting. It's like a more animal-istic side of him has taken over as he pushes me down to my knees, excitement overtaking some of the fear trapped inside me.

I stare up at him as his booted feet slowly circle me. Power exudes from every part of him as he towers over me. I shift slightly on my knees, never letting my gaze stray from him as he moves around me. I swear I see the glint of sharp canines in the glowing moonlight, but they're gone in an instant.

"Lift your arms for me, Wildcat," he growls. The no-nonsense request an order I comply with without thinking, I comply, raising them above me. "Good girl," he says as he rips my white dress over my head. Leaving me vulnerable to his penetrating inspection, he traces my every dip and curve with hungry eyes.

He softly skims his fingers across my lips before pushing two inside of my mouth, the unexpected intrusion gagging me, causing drool to drip down my chin. It is so dirty, so wrong, but I can't help but open my mouth further, welcoming him in. Pulling his fingers away, he unzips his black slacks, freeing himself.

I've never seen a man up close before. I lick my lips as he reveals himself to me. His cock is hard, thick and lengthy, and I have no idea how something of this size could cause anything but pain. Both nervous and eager, I'm willing to find out.

"Have you ever had a cock inside your pretty little mouth before, Little Seductress?"

They're his only words; my only warning before my mouth is full of him. I look up at him through my long lashes, as his hips slowly inch forward. Fingers fist through my hair, ensuring he has complete control over our movements.

My eyes widen as he pushes himself deep into my mouth, hitting the back of my throat. Tears spring to my eyes as I gag on his cock, unused to this punishing treatment. I'm sure my voice will be croaky tomorrow.

I don't know if I'm pushing him away or pulling him towards me as my nails bite into his thighs. Something inside me craves this, this euphoric high as he fucks my mouth relentlessly. Spit and saliva rolls down my chin as I choke on, unable to catch a breath. He finally relents, pulling back, just enough that I can heave in a sharp lungful of air before he pushes back inside my wanting mouth.

His head tilts back, and a groan escapes his lips. My core dampens with the carnal desire of such a depraved act as he quickens his pace.

"This wasn't quite the promise I made, was it?" He thuds down to his knees, shoving me the rest of the way to the hard ground along with him. His hand supports the back of my head, keeping me from further damage. A move in a polar opposite from the aggressive to the gentle that has me whimpering.

His fingers feather over my clit, and I pant. My cunt aching with an intensity I've never felt before. I start writhing as his fingers trail down to my entrance, one of his thick fingers pushing inside me with no resistance as his thumb takes over his persistent torment of my clit.

I grip his hand in my own, stopping him, the feeling too intense. He bats my hand away, chuckling as he continues his ministrations, pumping a second finger in alongside the first. I'm a whining mess, my pussy dripping juices down the crack of my arse as I squeeze around his fingers.

"So sensitive. It's okay, trust me."

Withdrawing his fingers, he slings my legs over his shoulders, lining himself up at my entrance. The tip of his length presses against me, and I whimper. His body leans further over mine, his weight pressing me deeper into the dry mud beneath me. My legs splay awkwardly, but I don't care as his lips touch mine in a deliciously soft kiss. Pulling back, he whispers softly.

"Next time, Wildcat."

I don't know if it's relief or bitter frustration I'm feeling. I ran, knowing the consequences of my actions would lead to this moment. Now he's holding back. His teeth graze my jaw and I give into the sensation, tilting my neck out in submission to him. Offering myself to him if only he would take it.

His grip on my hips is bruising as he slides his cock through my slick folds, and I let out a moan as he purposely slides against my engorged clit. My body is ready to explode, and I sense the rising orgasm as his fingers reach down to pinch my clit. The orgasm tears through me, my legs shaking uncontrollably, my body convulsing in overwhelming pleasure.

He rocks against me one last time, hot spurts of cum

shooting over me. I lay back panting out heaving breaths, more satisfied than I ever have before. As I lay there, the thin sheen of sweat beginning to cool on my body, I begin to shiver and start to sit up.

That's when he betrays me.

I know I should have expected it, but I'm disappointed. No, I'm more than disappointed. I'm angry. Not just at him, but at myself. I had known not to trust him, knowing this is what he did. When I feel the jab of the needle, I want to scream into the night air. It's too late, though. Darkness surrounds me too quickly, silver eyes forever watching.

CHAPTER 15

❧

RAFFERTY

Age Twenty-Six

I don't care if I look like a creep as I stare down at her beautiful face, unable to believe I have been so lucky at long last. As I trail my fingers through her auburn curls, I look down at her naked form and my cock stirs once again. I close my eyes tightly, desperate to gain control of my arousal.

My beast begs me to take her, to claim her fully. To ignore the consequences of this action. But I refuse to lose myself to him. It's taken me too long to get here to lose her trust now. Now I have my Wildcat, I won't let her go.

He growls within me, stalking back and forth, desperate to connect to what is his.

I know better.

For eight years, my beast and I have stalked her. Eight years we've trailed this clever seductress through this treacherous landscape. Keeping her safe from my brothers when the siren rings. It's been remarkable to watch her turn from a girl, already changed by circumstance, blossoming into the confident beauty she is now. A beauty who fights back, not only against capture from us but also against the coercion of the other women.

My Wildcat stands up for the new generations of girls who join the island and looks out for the well-being of the older of them. A shining beacon the others should match themselves to. If only the women all saw what she did. It is a mystery why they continue to allow Aggs to lead; she is a snake in their midst.

One who will lead them to their deaths.

Before she was even part of this twisted world, before my Wildcat ever stepped foot on Muliercula, Aggs made a discovery. A girl brought to the island merely months ahead of my little seductress had been a plant sent in by the doctors to spy on the other women.

A spy who was to report back information of how the women reacted to the more volatile of the drugs injected into their veins. To keep count of who lived, died and symptoms that presented. This girl disappeared within weeks of her assignment.

They made Aggs into the new contact.

For a while, it became hard for the doctors to get new girls onto the island. From what we had been told by our contact, they all died before they could be reached. If it hadn't been for my brave Wildcat; it never would have changed. The new girls would have kept on vanishing, disappearing into nothingness. Never to be seen again.

Maybe only to live in a worse fate.

Despite that, I am proud of her work, her fight and spirit. Her words keep these girls' hopes up, bringing forth a brighter future for them all despite the circumstances. The dynamics of Muliercula have changed since she arrived.

Part of that change has been in my brothers, some of whom have laid claim to obsessions of their own. Their mindsets changed, shifting to become something I once remembered. Less of violence and more of protection. I don't know what has caused this shift, but I am eternally grateful.

I pull my precious Wildcat onto my lap, letting her head rest on my shoulder. Her hair is a curtain of reddish-brown curls falling into her face. I push her locks from her angelic pale face and can't help the smile that forms on my lips. She has brought some sense of normality back to my once bleak life.

She is my everything, and I will do anything for her.

I know what must come next. It won't be easy and there will be severe consequences, but it'll be worth it in the end. My beast is in full agreement, prowling within me. He aches to do anything for our woman, our Wildcat, our seductress, our mate.

It won't be too much longer until we have to act.

Soon, one woman from Muliercula and seven men from Virilis will be chosen for my home. They plan for Aggs to be the next woman taken off this island. A perk of her little spy mission. I will not let that happen; she won't be leaving here alive.

I have other plans for who is to come to Venatio. My mouth tips into a smirk as I place a soft kiss on my little seductress' forehead.

One way or another, my Wildcat is coming home with me.

AFTERWORD

Thank you for reading and taking this dark journey with me. Writing a book has been something I've always wanted to do and never dreamed could possibly happen. So when my friends started to encourage me to go for it, I finally gave in, thinking why not.

I can't say it has always been easy, in fact I take my hat off to those who can get a book out every few weeks. But now my book baby is here and I'm so excited it has been shared with you all.

Look out for the next part of Nixi's story, coming soon.

PRONUNCIATION

Muliercula – mu.li'er.ku.la – meaning woman, hussy or minx in Latin.

Virilis – vi'ri.lis – meaning virile, manly and masculine.

Venatio – ve.na.tio – means hunting and chasing.

TRIGGER WARNINGS

This book contains graphic and violent scenes, that includes death and rape. On page sexual assault with a minor and including intent. Mentions of PTSD, anxiety and depression. Forced captivity, drug use and forced drug use. Sensory deprivation. Suggested cannibalism and body modifications.

Sexual scenes including, blood play, primal, MM and some self-love.

Do we even care that there's swearing at this point?

ACKNOWLEDGMENTS

Kristy, I legit would have never gotten this book out without you. You've been there with me basically holding my hand through it all. Your encouragement has meant the absolute world to me, and I cannot thank you enough. I promise never to steal Raeleen off of you. LOL. Love you!

To Momsy dearest, though you won't read the book, I'll let you have a peek at this page! You've supported this adventure since the beginning. Supporting me even as I procrastinated. Giving me *that* look if I wasn't writing. Especially if I hadn't done a job you asked of me because I was 'writing.' Now you get to sit through me writing the next few books... enjoy! I LOVE YOU!

Lilly, you were the one who made this a prequel, who got this book as complex as it is and got me *showing* more of the background. Basically you made this book how dark it is. Thank you so much guiding me through.

To everyone who helped read, support, and cheer me

on; I thank you all. I appreciate each and every one of you so much.

STALK ISLA HARDING

AMAZON

GOODREADS

FACEBOOK

FACEBOOK READER GROUP

TIKTOK

INSTAGRAM

Printed in Great Britain
by Amazon